Laurel Canyon

Howard Drew Novels, Volume 5

Larry Darter

Published by Larry Darter, 2024.

LAUREL CANYON

First edition. May 14, 2024.

ISBN: 979-8987694466

Written by Larry Darter.

Table of Contents

Chapter One...1

Chapter Two...5

Chapter Three 11

Chapter Four 16

Chapter Five 21

Chapter Six 27

Chapter Seven 32

Chapter Eight..36

Chapter Nine..39

Chapter Ten 45

Chapter Eleven..50

Chapter Twelve 55

Chapter Thirteen 60

Chapter Fourteen 66

Chapter Fifteen 69

Chapter Sixteen 72

Chapter Seventeen 75

Chapter Eighteen..78

Chapter Nineteen..82

Chapter Twenty 86

Chapter Twenty-One 89

Chapter Twenty-Two...93

Chapter Twenty-Three 97

Chapter Twenty-Four...101

Chapter Twenty-Five 105

Chapter Twenty-Six..108

Chapter Twenty-Seven..111

Chapter Twenty-Eight...115

Chapter Twenty-Nine 119

Chapter Thirty 123

Chapter Thirty-One..128

Chapter Thirty-Two..131

Chapter Thirty-Three..134

Chapter Thirty-Four 141
Chapter Thirty-Five 145
Chapter Thirty-Six 149
Chapter Thirty-Seven 152
Chapter Thirty-Eight 159
Chapter Thirty-Nine 163
Chapter Forty 166
Chapter Forty-One 172
Chapter Forty-Two 176
Chapter Forty-Three 179
Chapter Forty-Four 183
Chapter Forty-Five 186
Chapter Forty-Six 191

For Tom, with thanks

Chapter One

IT WAS ABOUT HALF-PAST six in the evening, and the sun had receded behind the Mulholland hills. Driving west from Laurel Canyon Boulevard, Drew wound his way up several narrow streets toward the scene.

While still considered a pricey section of Los Angeles, the Laurel Canyon area homes were older, and the narrow streets were more congested with parked cars than other exclusive LA neighborhoods. With the houses crowded together on smallish residential lots, room for driveways and garages was at a premium, making options other than street parking almost nonexistent.

Drew spotted the news trucks as he neared the Wonderland location, large television units and larger trucks with lighting equipment. The media had come out in full force after monitoring police radio frequencies and learning something big was going on. The ubiquitous media vehicles blocked all the streets near the scene and surrounding area. There appeared no way in or out, so Drew pulled his unmarked Ford Crown Victoria to the curb two blocks down the street and got out.

As he approached the front of the property, festooned with yellow crime-scene tape, a reporter spotted him and jogged towards him, shouting questions. In moments, barely out of his car, a dozen or more reporters besieged him. The first one shouted, "Detective, you need to talk to all of us." Ignoring them, Drew walked to the uniformed officer securing the scene, leaned against the fender of his black and white Ford Explorer.

The patrol cop, an obvious gym rat with tanned skin and close-cropped, sun-bleached blond hair, straightened up as he approached. To Drew, the cop looked like a surfer dude caricature out of one of Joseph Wambaugh's novels. The name plate above the cop's breast pocket said his name was Knox. He looked at Drew through Oakley shades, though it was going on dusk.

"Howard Drew," Knox said, with the surprise clear in his voice. "When did you get on RHD?"

Drew looked at him a moment before answering. He didn't know Knox, but that meant nothing. Every cop in Hollywood Division probably knew Drew's story.

"Couple of weeks ago," Drew said.

"This is your first one in the RHD saddle?"

Drew fished out a pack of smokes, took one out, and lit it.

"Something like that. Who's here?"

"Chadwick and some other Hollywood detectives and Estrada and some Asian chick from RHD."

"Li?"

"Whatever."

Drew caught the contempt in the cop's voice, but made no reply. It didn't matter that he knew Amy Li was a first-rate investigator, since that would mean nothing to Knox. Guys like Knox saw the only reason he was wearing a blue suit instead of carrying a gold detective's shield was that he was a white male in the era of DEI hiring and promotion. It was the sort of festering bad feelings best ignored. Knox evidently interpreted Drew's nonresponse as disagreement and continued.

"Anyway, besides them, the medical examiner investigator and the SID techs are inside."

Drew dropped the half-smoked cigarette on the pavement and ground it out with the toe of his shoe.

"What about Lieutenant Moreno?"

"Nope."

Drew took the proffered clipboard with the crime scene log attached and signed in. Then, without another word to Knox, he lifted the yellow plastic tape and walked under it towards the death house, a two-story, white stucco townhouse above a garage. It was a warm, humid early July evening and after leaving the air-conditioned Crown Vic, Drew already felt the sweat on his skin beneath his shirt. As he walked up the short driveway and stepped onto the sidewalk, the Hollywood detective, Reece Chadwick, approached him. He gave Drew the short version of what he had already observed before Estrada and Li arrived.

Chadwick looked Drew in the eye and stated, "Looks like someone walked through the house with buckets of blood and sloshed it everywhere."

Drew followed the detective up the common staircase from the street level shared with the house next door until a narrow brick wall divided the stairs. They arrived at the front door, which faced the entrance to the neighboring house just a few feet away. Li and a tall, lean black man wearing what was obviously an expensive, tailored suit, were standing outside the door on the landing.

"Howie, where have you been?" Li quipped with a smirk.

"I had to fight forty-five minutes of holiday getaway traffic on the Ventura Highway and drive like a madman to get here," Drew said. "You been waiting long?"

"We got here about twenty minutes ago," Li said. "We haven't been inside yet." Gesturing to the black detective, she continued. "This is Detective Estrada. I don't think you've met."

Drew nodded, looked at Estrada, and extended his hand. The detectives shook.

"Howard Drew. My friends call me Howie. Good to meet you."

"I'm Oscar, and likewise, Howie," Estrada said with a slight Latino accent. Drew had heard of Estrada and knew he was of Afro-Cuban heritage. Drew turned to Chadwick, who had been the first detective on the scene.

"This isn't going to screw up my Fourth of July weekend plans, is it?"

Chadwick grimaced. "My head is still spinning from what I saw inside, Howie," he said.

Judging from his reaction, Drew picked up the vibe and put on his game face.

"I'll brief you as we go," Chadwick said to the RHD detectives. "It's going to be a long evening." He handed out vinyl boot covers and latex gloves all around. "Put on your booties and glove up and we'll get started."

Drew, Li, and Estrada slipped the covers over the soles of their footwear and pulled on the latex gloves. Compared to Estrada, Drew supposed he was a little underdressed in his polo shirt, jeans, and Merrell hiking boots. But department policy permitted responding to call-outs in casual clothing and Drew had been visiting a friend, not at home with access to a suit, when he took the call from Moreno anyway. It wasn't something he was worried about.

Drew followed Chadwick inside, followed by Li and Estrada. This was the first high-profile case Drew and Li would work together since getting assigned to Homicide Special. Accustomed to each other's tactics and idiosyncrasies, they always seemed on the same page. Estrada was the wild card since neither of them had ever worked with the detective before, but Drew assumed he was a competent investigator since he had earned an assignment to the legendary LAPD Homicide Special section.

Drew figured he had seen it all and was prepared for the worst. And the moment he entered the house, he saw it was.

Chapter Two

CHADWICK KNEW THE ROUTE to take and moved left into the living room area. Drew's senses fired on all cylinders. He knew being observant was the key to a good crime scene investigation.

Chadwick moved slowly, pointing out everything he had already seen. The RHD detectives took in everything in their path as Chadwick directed the walk through, avoiding the blood that pooled on the floor. All three of the Homicide Special detectives made mental notes as they evaluated the scene. Drew knew he would guide their boss, Lieutenant Moreno, as well as scientific investigation division techs, through the grisly scene. At that time, the documentation of the scene would begin in earnest.

A white female who looked to Drew to be in her twenties lay face down alongside a floral-patterned sofa. A previously hanging potted plant was lying on the floor near her body, a clear unintended target of someone swinging an unknown type of weapon meant for the young woman. She lay with her head atop her outstretched right arm. Blood had pooled and soaked into the fabric of the sofa where her head had apparently been at the time the assault began. Someone had then either pulled her from the sofa or she had rolled off it onto the floor during the beating. Blood castoff, splatter from the weapon, tailed up the wall and was evident on the ceiling.

The blood spatter not only showed the ferocity of the attack, it also told the detectives that someone had continually beaten the victim while she lay on the floor with overhand blows from a blunt instrument.

On the wall to the left of the sofa, Drew noticed a faint swipe-type blood transfer left on the electric switch plate for the overhead lights. It appeared someone with blood on their hand had attempted to manipulate the switch to the on or the off position. Drew noted the lights were off.

Several SID technicians worked busily throughout the downstairs portion of the split-level townhouse, under the direction of other Hollywood detectives. As the detectives walked toward the narrow staircase, criminalist

Abby Herrera summoned them over. She had found something interesting on a wall next to the stairs in the stairwell. About halfway up the staircase, Herrera pointed out what appeared to be fresh marks on the drywall about two feet above the stairs, a small striation pattern indented in the wall. Tiny areas of blood spatter showed on the wall bearing the indentation.

The detectives continued upstairs and entered a bedroom. A white male victim, late thirties to early forties, lay supine on the bed with a comforter covering the body from the feet to the chest. The pulverized head of the victim was lying on a blood-soaked pillow. It appeared someone had attacked him while the victim slept. Overturned furniture, dumped drawers, and the contents spilled from the almost empty closet showed someone had ransacked the room. Blood splattered the basin in the en suite bathroom where it looked like someone has used the sink to clean up.

"There was a second victim found in this room on the floor, a white female," Chadwick said, pointing to an area drenched in blood on the floor in the northeast corner. "When the first patrol units arrived, she was still alive and an RA unit transported her to Cedars-Sinai. But she was circling the drain and probably won't survive."

The walls, carpet, and bedding in the room were all soaked in blood. Drew thought the room liked like a slaughterhouse.

"She was probably lying there for hours before the paramedics arrived," Chadwick said.

"How the hell did she survive?" Li asked in wonder. "She must have lost three or four pints of blood."

Chadwick continued his guided tour of the room. Detectives noted additional bloody castoff from a weapon up the walls and on the ceiling. A hypodermic needle lay in an open drawer of a nightstand beside the bed along with a narcotics injection kit, known as a fit, resting beside an open pack of unfiltered Pall Mall cigarettes on a nearby dresser.

"The Pall Malls tell me this guy was an ex-con," Chadwick said. "And a hype for sure based on the narcotics paraphernalia."

Drew nodded in agreement.

Chadwick led the group out of the bedroom and upstairs to the third level to a second bedroom. "It gets worse," he announced as they entered the room. In a sitting position, leaning against the lower half of a television cart, was the beaten and bloodied body of a white male in his forties. From the position of the body, and that the victim wore pants and shoes, it looked like something had roused him from bed just before the attack.

"Looks like he put up a fight," Li said.

"But the bad guys won," Estrada noted.

Drew saw the victim's head had experienced extensive trauma.

"This is the fifth victim," Chadwick said, gesturing to the battered corpse of a white female lying partially off the bed in the room, her skull so badly crushed she was unrecognizable and she was lying in a pool of blood. Besides the bed, blood was evident behind the television cart, and throughout the entire room. Footwear impressions superimposed over one another in the blood pooled on the floor showed there were multiple assailants. Blowflies buzzed annoyingly around the room.

"What a fucking mess," Drew said in disgust.

"The suspects ransacked this room like the other bedroom," Chadwick said. "They were definitely searching for something."

The detectives also noted more drug paraphernalia present in the room.

"This was personal," Estrada said. "They must have pissed someone off. Or it was a drug rip-off."

"Were they users or dealers?" Li asked no one in particular.

"A buddy of mine in narcotics called me just before you guys arrived," Chadwick said to Li. "He heard the radio call and called to tell me this is a known drug house. They slung dope out of here, mostly heroine and crack, and were all players according to narcotics."

"We know who they are?" Drew asked.

"Not officially yet," Chadwick said, consulting his notebook. "But according to my source, we have a pretty good idea. These two are probably Harlan Tate and his girlfriend, Nancy Poole. They had the lease on the place. The guy in the other bedroom is probably Joe Allen and the survivor, his wife Dawn Allen. We think the young woman downstairs is Amanda Quinn."

"What's the affiliation?" Li asked.

"The drug guys call them the Wonderland gang. Joe Allen was the leader. Allen and Tate were outlaw bikers, ex-cons who moved narcotics for one of the Mexican cartels. And according to my buddy, narcotics suspects they supplemented their drug dealing earnings with burglaries and armed robberies of rival drug dealers."

"So, maybe they didn't pay their suppliers," Li said.

"This doesn't feel like a cartel thing," Estrada said. "They left no *narcomensajes*, messages identifying the killers, so named to indicate a drug-related killing and to serve as a warning to others."

"Maybe it was a revenge thing by someone they ripped off, some rival drug dealers," Drew said. "This is overkill."

"Could be," Chadwick agreed. "That would explain why it looks personal. Blunt force trauma all around. Someone making a point."

Drew glanced at Estrada, who was holding a handkerchief over his nose. Their eyes met.

"Howie, let's get the hell out of here," Estrada said, his voice muffled by the handkerchief. "This is pure rotten dead people we're inhaling."

Drew nodded, and the detectives trouped back downstairs and out the front door. They took the exterior stairs back down to street level.

"Sorry to bigfoot you, Chadwick," Drew said. "But this is going to be high profile, so Homicide Special will probably take it."

Chadwick grinned. "Four on the floor? No problem, Drew. You can have it and welcome."

"Thanks. We could still use some help from your guys."

"Sure, whatever you need."

Drew thanked him and turned to Li and Estrada.

"So, what's the plan, Howie?" Li asked. "You're the three." She smiled and winked.

"Anybody talk to Moreno?" Drew asked. Moreno had called him and he had called Li. But he hadn't called Estrada, so he was curious about it.

"I did," Estrada said. "He called me and told me to come and help you guys because it came out as a multi-five murder scene."

"Is he coming out?" Drew asked. "He didn't say when he called me."

"He was halfway up to his lake cabin to spend the holiday weekend," Estrada said. "He said he was going to drop his family off at the cabin first, so he's at least an hour and a half from us."

"Okay, I'll call him and let him know what we've got," Drew said. "Oscar, you marshal a team of patrol officers and Hollywood detectives and start a thorough canvass of the vicinity outside the house and the neighborhood, looking for witnesses or evidence. Make sure everyone documents everything in writing and have anything photographed you think necessary. You know the drill. Check out all parked cars and note the license plate numbers, check the garbage cans and any areas where the suspects might have discarded evidence."

Drew turned to Amy. "I want you inside working with the SID technicians. After I call Moreno, I'll take a videographer. I'm going to shoot the entire crime scene starting out here and then moving inside."

Estrada and Li both nodded and went their separate ways. Chadwick went with Estrada to help coordinate the Hollywood response. Drew took out his phone and called Lieutenant Moreno. He answered on the second ring.

"Lou Moreno."

"It's Drew. I called to update you."

"What have we got?"

"Home invasion. Four dead bodies and one critically injured, a female. An RA unit transported her before the Hollywood detectives arrived, and Reese Chadwick told me she was probably circling the drain. All blunt-force trauma."

"How bad?"

"You ever look through the Tate–LaBianca murder book? This might top it."

"Jesus."

"You coming out?"

"I just got to my cabin for the weekend. You need me there?"

"Up to you, Lieutenant. We have it under control."

"All right. I'll be back early, but I'm not coming down there tonight. I'll probably just roll to the PAB sometime tomorrow."

"Okay, catch you there," Drew said. "We'll be here all night."

"You know when it happened?"

"Judging from the scene, I'm guessing early this morning or late last night. I think it's at least twelve hours old. But I'm speculating based on the decomp and blood evidence."

"Okay, Drew. I know you know how to do your job. I'll see at the office sometime tomorrow."

"You got it, Lieutenant."

Moreno disconnected, and Drew put his phone in his pocket. Then he climbed the stairs to find a videographer.

Chapter Three

AS DREW MOVED THROUGH the crime scene with the criminalist and his shoulder mounted video camera, he did the major narration, although SID technicians commented when appropriate along the way. In just over two hours, they had captured the entire crime scene, including the bludgeoned bodies *in situ*. Drew wanted the video mostly for investigative purposes, but knew the prosecutor could use some of the footage later in court. The camera captured the raw violence visited upon the victims in the starkest of terms. It also brought to life the relationships between the victims and other evidence at the scene. Drew, his team, and the criminalists continued the investigation throughout the night and into the next day.

Well into the night, Drew received word from the hospital that victim Dawn Allen was still unconscious but alive. She had undergone extensive surgery by a world-class neurosurgeon at Cedars-Sinai whose work had probably improved her chances of survival greatly. Dawn Allen remained under twenty-four-hour guard by the LAPD.

As night turned to morning, Drew and his team hardly noticed. They had worked nonstop for hours, trying to identify and document every bit of potential evidence present in the monster crime scene. Estrada had found and removed two Galil ACE Israeli rifles, weapons manufactured in Colombia that were becoming increasingly popular with Mexican drug cartels. He booked them into evidence, even though the detectives knew of no connection between the murders and the use of any firearms. Everything the detectives observed they documented in writing.

By early afternoon on July second, all three detectives were exhausted. As the outside temperature rose, so did the temperature inside the house and it had climbed to over one hundred degrees. They had to keep all the windows closed since they couldn't alter anything at the scene from its original state until they concluded the investigation. They hadn't used the central air conditioning or fans present in the house.

The detectives cleared only one evidence free area in the living room to make their lengthy stay at the crime scene more bearable and used a small table and chairs from the breakfast nook as workspace. Several of the SID people continued moving about, dusting for prints, measuring, photographing, and collecting potential evidence.

No one would move any of the victims until the investigators finished documenting all the evidence, and the coroner's investigators had completed their independent scene investigation to their satisfaction. Only then would they call for coroner vans to remove the bodies.

The blowflies, known as DB or dead body flies, buzzed throughout the house, drawn to the stench of the decomposing human bodies. The house reeked of the odor of the decaying remains, a smell impossible to ignore. And as all veteran homicide investigators knew, whatever you smelled, you also tasted, and that was a very unpleasant experience at a murder scene. The oppressive hot conditions inside the house sped up the decomposition process and intensified the foul odors.

When Lieutenant Lou Moreno had arrived at the PAB and learned Drew and his team were still processing the scene, he had driven out to the murder house on Wonderland Avenue. There he had run the gauntlet of impatient reporters like they were the paparazzi on his way inside the house. Drew, now intimately familiar with the scene, had given his supervisor a far more robust guided tour than the initial walk through Reece Chadwick had given him and his team when they had arrived over twenty-four hours earlier.

"You weren't exaggerating, Drew," Moreno said after they had completed the tour. "I believe this scene is even worse than the Tate–LaBianca murder scene. You think this was over a narcotics trafficking beef?"

"I think narcotics may be involved, LT, but I feel there was more to it than only that. A narcotics officer who spoke to Chadwick said these people were running drugs smuggled over the border by one of the Tijuana cartels, and as Oscar observed during our walk through yesterday, this doesn't feel like a cartel thing. No one here got shot or cut. Someone bludgeoned these people to death using something like steel pipes and hammers."

"I hope it wasn't a cartel thing," Moreno said. "I want, the captain wants, and the chief wants these murders cleared by arrests, eventually. If a cartel did this, the suspects would have long since gone back across the border and, with the rampant corruption in Mexico, they would be far beyond our reach now."

"Well, we have ruled nothing out, but I'm skeptical about cartel involvement."

"You made next of kin notifications yet?"

"No, Sir. We're still waiting on positive identifications. SID found identification here in the house suggesting the victims are who we think they are. But I'm holding off on the notifications until we have positive identifications."

"Looks like you have things well in hand, Detective. No surprise. I know what you can do. I'm confident you and each member of your team will conduct this investigation professionally and thoroughly and most of all will deliver the results I and the chief of police expect."

Drew only nodded. He knew you could never count on results, no matter how hard you worked. Every case was different, and past performance did not guarantee future results. That explained why the current city-wide average homicide clearance rate hovered at around seventy-six percent.

"You going to make a statement to the press, Lieutenant?" he asked. "They've hung around us like vultures since the moment we arrived."

"I'm going home to shower, shave, and change clothes first," Moreno said. "Then I'll return and take them on." Moreno turned to leave, pausing and turning his head to speak. "Keep me informed on your progress, Detective."

Drew nodded again. "Copy that, Sir."

Drew stood on the landing outside the front door and watched Moreno move down the stairs. Dozens of media folks, some roused from napping, leaped to their feet and hurried towards him. The lieutenant ignored their shouted questions and shouted back. "No comment at this time. I will be back to give a press release later this evening." He then strode to his police ride and climbed in. And, much to the chagrin of the members of the press, drove away.

Two hours after leaving the scene, Lieutenant Moreno returned to give a statement to the press. As soon as he got out of his vehicle, the media crowded around him like starving dogs after the last bone. Moreno looked like he had just stepped off the cover of a men's fashion magazine—dressed in a tailored suit, shaved, and with his gray hair perfectly coiffed. The questions came fast and furious, but Moreno was a pro, adept at answering questions without giving out any actual information that could compromise the investigation.

After answering a few general questions, the lieutenant delivered a brief statement lacking any solid details. He stated the LAPD had identified the victims, but wouldn't release their names until they had notified the victim's next of kin. Moreno had followed rule number one about dealing with the press during a murder investigation perfectly. Always tell them something, but never give them anything.

As evening fell, four coroner's examiners arrived in two vans from the Los Angeles County Coroner's Office. The reporters appreciated their arrival. They knew that soon the transport teams would roll out the four bodies and they would finally get something solid for the late evening news.

The investigators entered the townhouse and went about the grisly task of photographing each dead body up close in the presence of the detectives. They then inserted thermometers in the abdominal area and liver of each of the deceased to determine internal body temperature. The battered conditions of the victims aside, the unforgettable stench was intense. The liver temperature readings were consistent and revealed that death had occurred in the very early hours of July first.

Once the coroner's team completed their work, the transport team put the victims into black body bags, strapped them to gurneys, and carried them downstairs. At street level, they rolled the gurneys to the vans, loaded the bodies, and left for the coroner's office on North Mission Road in Los Angeles.

Drew, Li, and Estrada assessed the scene one last time as the SID criminalists prepared to spray ninhydrin throughout the entire premises to draw out any latent palm prints or fingerprints pit of porous interior surfaces. An LAPD cartographer worked on composing schematics of the entire residence, inside and out, all to scale. The detectives understood they would probably return to the crime scene again, but realized defense attorneys would probably scrutinize thoroughly any subsequent work they did at the scene. This had been the one and only time that they would have complete control over the crime scene.

Four hours later, it was a wrap at the townhouse on Wonderland Avenue. The sun had set again. The detectives secured the house as best they could and affixed crime scene warning stickers across the front door jamb along with crime scene tape.

Standing outside the house on the street, the three weary detectives discussed the next steps in their investigation. Rest was high on the list since they had gone without sleep for over thirty-six hours. As they walked to their rides, the remaining reporters with cameras rolling descended on them. Several shouted questions, talking over one another. The detectives kept walking, ignoring the questions and pleas for comment. Once inside their vehicles with the windows up, they all drove away into the night.

Chapter Four

DREW HAD GIVEN LI AND Escobar permission to report two hours late to make certain they got adequate rest. But it was still early morning on day three when Drew and his team assembled at their desks on the fifth floor of the Police Administration Building or the PAB, as the cops called LAPD Headquarters on West First Street.

Lieutenant Moreno had supplied them with additional help. He had tasked two, two-person Homicide Special detective teams to make the next of kin notifications, now that they had positive identification on all four homicide victims. The phones rang nonstop, and Moreno had also assigned a few more detectives to help Drew and the team with the tip line.

Drew had provided the detectives handling the phones with a few facts known only to the killers and the police about the murders. They used these facts, called "investigative keys", for elimination purposes when talking with callers. As with all high-profile cases, Drew knew there were always cranks who called the tip lines wishing to confess to the crime even though they had no involvement.

Estrada worked on completing the background checks on the victims. It was an essential part of profiling them. Delving into their backgrounds might reveal leads to additional motives or other facts crucial to identifying their killers.

In response to Estrada's inquiries, the LAPD Records and Identification Division had revealed that Joe Allen and Harlan Tate had extensive criminal records in the state of California. Both had several arrests and convictions for robbery, assault, drug dealing, and possession of narcotics. Nancy Poole had a drug possession case pending in the Los Angeles County court system. Dawn Allen and Amanda Quinn had no criminal records. Estrada had also learned that Joe Allen had been a strong suspect in the murder of a well-known Los Angeles sports promoter whose bullet-riddled body had been discovered by police in the trunk of his car, which had been left in a parking structure at Universal City Studios.

Drew had tasked Li with keeping tabs on Dawn Allen's condition at Cedars-Sinai Hospital. She kept in touch with the officers of Metro Division, an elite division of the Los Angeles Police Department under its Special Operations Group, tasked with keeping the day and night watch on Allen at the hospital to protect her against the possibility of someone wanting to complete the Wonderland slaughter. Metro had orders to detain any visitor who showed up asking to see Allen other than vetted immediate family members and to notify Li so that the detectives could interview such persons immediately.

Drew worked on assembling four murder books, one for each victim. While most of a homicide detective's investigative work product was now computerized at the LAPD, Drew preferred to build physical murder books the old school way, using the blue three-ring binders. When he had first began as a homicide investigator, his mentor had insisted on it and Drew had adopted the practice because he preferred it. It involved some duplication of effort, but often Drew took murder books home with him after working hours to review the information for the third or fourth time to make certain he didn't overlook the smallest detail that could prove crucial to the case. He preferred the binders because he could remove all the reports, witness statements, interviews, and crime scene photos and spread them out on his dining room table to study. Drew found it preferable to have everything right in front of him rather than looking at things piecemeal on a computer screen.

As the team leader, Drew's primary responsibility was to push the investigation forward. He knew murder investigations were like sharks and had to keep moving or die. He would also maintain the physical murder books by inserting the required documents in the binders and would maintain the "chrono," the chronological record of the investigation.

Report writing was Li's strength and Drew would rely on her to handle that and to draft any search warrant applications that became necessary. He had already tasked Estrada with completing the background investigations associated with the case and would also have him keeping track of the evidence and the eventual reports received from the labs processing the collected evidence.

It was late afternoon after Drew, Li, and Estrada had long since returned to work after their lunch break when one detective handling the phones rang Drew's desk phone. "I've got someone on the phone you need you to talk to," the detective said. "All he would give me as a name is an alias, Tiny Tim."

Drew assumed a crank had slipped past the detective, but he told him to transfer the call to him.

Li smiled when Drew identified himself and said into the phone, "Hey, look. Nicknames are fine, but I need your actual name if we're going to talk."

The caller responded with, "Timothy Johnson."

"Okay, Mr. Johnson, what can I do for you?"

"I'm with someone who has important information on the murders at Laurel Canyon, and it can't wait. He's a friend of mine and says his girlfriend, one of the victims, was staying at the house when it all went down."

"Do you know the girlfriend's name?"

"Yeah, she goes by Mandy. But I think her actual name is Amanda. Amanda Quinn."

"All right, Mr. Johnson. Can you bring your friend here to talk to us at police headquarters on West First?"

"See, I can't really do that. I have this thing pending with the LA District Attorney's office and I don't want to get arrested. I'm hoping to get some consideration on it for helping you guys with your investigation."

"Okay, we can discuss your situation later. Tell me where you are and we'll come to you."

"At the house."

"What house? Your home?"

"No, you know... where it happened."

"On Wonderland?"

"Yeah, where the murders happened."

"Listen carefully, Mr. Johnson. We're on the way. Stay where you are. Got it?"

"Yeah, we'll be waiting."

Drew hung up. He glanced at Li and then Estrada. "Let's go!" He grabbed his jacket off his chair and stood up, explaining the phone call to his partners on their way out the door.

Once again, the sun was setting behind the hills as the detectives arrived at the townhouse on Wonderland Avenue. They found a lone male seated in an older Cadillac Escalade parked at the curb directly in front of the townhouse. Drew walked to the back of the vehicle and called out. "Timothy?"

Johnson acknowledged him and got out of the Escalade and walked back to Drew and Estrada, who had joined him. Estrada stepped forward and patted Johnson down casually for weapons. Li remained between the front of Drew's police ride and the Cadillac with her hand resting on the grip of her holstered Glock, providing cover for the contact. It didn't surprise Drew that the nickname Tiny Tim didn't fit. It never did. Johnson looked like a former USC offensive lineman gone to seed with a large belly hanging over his belt. Drew figured the man stood six foot three and weighed well over three hundred pounds.

"So, Tim, where's your friend?" Drew asked.

"He's in the house. I told him it wasn't a good idea, but he's stubborn."

Drew and Estrada eyed each other. Then, an LAPD black and white Ford Explorer happened by, with two officers handling a radio call in the neighborhood. They had stopped when they recognized Drew and Estrada as detectives. Drew told them to notify communications detectives needed their assistance at the location.

"We've got a guy inside the house we need to confront," he explained.

The two officers nodded.

"Keep an eye on this guy and run him and his plate while we check out the house."

"You got it, Detective," one officer acknowledged.

Drew, Li, and Estrada drew their weapons and headed up the stairs to the front door. When they arrived at the landing, they saw someone had removed the crime scene seal from the door jamb and the door stood open a crack. The lights were on in the house. They heard scuffling sounds coming from inside, revealing someone was moving around.

Drew pushed the door open and announced them. "LAPD. Anyone here?" Then the detectives hit the door.

Chapter Five

MOVING TOWARD THE KITCHEN where the noise emanated from, a curious sight met the detectives when they entered the room. A white male around forty years of age who looked like a biker was on all fours, gathering up what appeared to be pills and tablets from the floor and stuffing them into his pockets. Both Drew and Estrada shouted at him to stop what he was doing and to show them his hands. But the man seemed oblivious to them, continuing to crawl around on the floor, gathering up the narcotics like a squirrel gathering acorns for the winter. Estrada shouted louder, his Glock pointed at the intruder, and seemed to get through to him. The stocky man stopped his frenzied activity and glanced over his shoulder at the detectives. Slowly, he got to his feet and turned toward them. He had longish, dirty blonde hair and wore a sleeveless denim jacket over a black T-shirt, jeans, and leather boots. A chain attached the wallet in his rear pocket to his belt, biker style.

The man appeared upset, even distraught, but wasn't combative. Estrada holstered his weapon, searched the man for weapons, and handcuffed him.

"You entered a crime scene," Drew said to the man. "You're under arrest."

Estrada had pulled the man's wallet out of his pocket, looking for identification.

"My old lady was here during the attack," the man said. "I wanted to find out how she was and what hospital they took her to."

"You're Dennis Mack?" Estrada asked, looking at the California license he had found the man's wallet.

"That's right, bro," Mack replied. "You guys know where Mandy is?"

"Amanda Quinn?"

"Yeah, man. That's my old lady. She was here. I saw on the news she survived and I want to know what hospital she's in."

Drew knew the local news had reported there was a hospitalized female survivor of the attack, but not the woman's name, since the LAPD hadn't revealed Dawn Allen's identity to the press. Mack had assumed the woman

21

the press had alluded to was his girlfriend. He withheld from Mack the fact that Amanda Quinn was dead. He wanted to get him into a more controlled environment before telling him.

"We're going to transport you to the Hollywood station for questioning," Drew advised Mack. "And we'll try to answer your questions about your girlfriend when we get there."

Mack didn't seem to have any objections, although it wouldn't have mattered anyway. Estrada took Mack by one of his handcuffed arms and escorted him out of the house and down the stairs, with Drew and Li in tow.

Back on the street, a uniformed officer approached Drew.

"The registration on the Escalade comes back to Timothy Johnson with a West Hollywood address," the officer said. "He has an active county misdemeanor warrant. You want me to confirm it and hook him up?"

"No, we're handling something more important right now," Drew said. "We'll address his warrant later."

Drew walked over to Johnson, who was eyeing his handcuffed buddy.

"You arresting Denny?"

"That's right. The house is still a crime scene. He ignored the warning stickers and forced his way inside. He's going to the Hollywood station with us. But if he cooperates and answers our questions, we might work something out. You're welcome to follow us down and wait to see if he gets kicked."

"Okay, I'll do that."

Drew told the patrol cops they could get back to their call while Estrada put Mack in the back seat of Drew's ride. He got in the back beside Mack while Drew and Li got in the front. Drew started the car, and they headed to the Hollywood station, with Johnson following.

Upon their arrival at the Hollywood station, the detectives escorted Mack to an interview room. Drew removed the handcuffs and put Mack in a straight-backed metal chair on one side of the small metal table in the room. Li took Mack's California driver's license from Estrada and left the room to run background checks on the man through local and federal sources. The small, drab room, furnished with only the table and four metal chairs, projected the image that the room was for business only. Drew and Estrada sat down across the table from Mack.

"You said you would tell me about my old lady," Mack said, eyeing Drew. He had been nervous and had asked about Amanda Quinn during the entire ride to the station. "How bad did she get hurt?"

Drew got straight down to business. Mack was a badass biker, emotionally charged, and who had probably been in and out of jail his entire life. Drew needed Mack to be straight with them, so he would be straight with him. "I'm sorry, but she didn't make it. Amanda was the first person killed when the intruders entered the house. They beat her to death."

Mack jumped to his feet, knocking over his chair, cursing and howling, his face a mask of both rage and pain. Estrada also sprang to his feet and started around the table.

"They said on the news there was a woman survivor," Mack shouted. "It has to be Mandy. She did nothing to anyone to deserve to get killed." Sobbing, he croaked, "Why?"

Drew, still sitting in his chair, replied calmly. "We're hoping you can tell us why, and who? Sit down, Dennis."

Mack jerked his chair upright and sat down heavily, his elbows on the table and his face in his hands. Then he reached into his jacket pocket, pulled out a pill, and showed it to the cops. "See this? It's a fucking quaalude!" Then he popped the pill into his mouth and swallowed as Drew and Estrada looked at him in astonishment.

Mack reached into the pocket again and cast a handful of assorted pills and capsules onto the table. He picked up a capsule and held it up. "See this? It's a rainbow." Then he popped the capsule into his mouth and swallowed. Estrada, uncomfortable with what he was watching, looked at Drew, who just shook his head, signaling Estrada not to intervene. Mack selected another pill from the table.

"This one is a red devil," he said, popping it in his mouth.

"Drew?" Estrada said, clearly growing more and more unsettled and nervous about the spectacle he was witnessing.

Drew held up a hand to Estrada. He knew it was unconventional to allow a prisoner to consume drugs during an interview, but he wanted Mack to talk and figured he would clam up if they confronted him over the narcotics. And he knew the man was only expressing his rage and grief the only way he knew how at the moment.

Mack jumped back to his feet again, cursing.

"Sit down, Dennis," Drew commanded. "And chill, or we'll handcuff you to the damn chair." Mack complied, sinking back down on the chair.

"He's taking drugs in a police station," Estrada said to Drew. "This guy is dangerous."

Drew smiled at Estrada to console him. "He's ready to talk, and I want to hear what he has to say. I can handle him. I don't want to jam you up on this. Why don't you go get him a cup of coffee?"

Estrada eyed Drew as though he were insane, but then he walked to the door and went out. Drew turned back to Mack. Unless the guy did something completely crazy like trying to take an entire handful of pills or getting combative, he would let the situation ride. While tasteless, he intended to exploit the death of the biker's girlfriend to learn what Mack knew. It seemed clear the biker was a key to what had gone down at the house on Wonderland and Drew wasn't about to risk ending up with nothing.

Li entered the interview room with the cup of coffee Drew had sent Estrada after. She put the cup down on the table in front of Mack. He picked it up and sipped the hot brew greedily, seemingly appreciative the coffee gave him something else to think about than the business at hand and the death of his girlfriend.

Li passed several sheets of paper to Drew, Mack's rap sheet. She couldn't take her eyes off the pills and capsules scattered on the table. Drew looked at the papers. A cursory glance showed Dennis Mack had arrests and convictions for burglary, robbery, auto theft, drug possession, and dealing. And that was just the first page. He noticed Sacramento PD had made several of the entries. Drew had spent some time there growing up and was familiar with the area. He decided to use that to try to build rapport with Mack.

"Hey, Dennis, you know Doc and Crow, a couple of lightweight Hell's Angels?" Drew asked.

"Yeah, I know those dudes from Sacto. Shit, they rode with Bobby Parker out of Oakland for a while."

Drew nodded, feeling this was a way of connecting.

"They used to hang out in West Sac to stay away from the downtown cops, didn't they?" Drew continued.

"They weren't hiding from the Sacto cops. They were chasing young tail and looking for weed in West Sac. Both were easier to find on that side of the river."

The banter was reminiscent of two guys raised in the same town but on opposite sides of the street.

Drew made a show of looking down at the rap sheet again now that he had Mack talking. He shook his head and eyed the biker. "Wow, looks like you've been a bad dude, Dennis."

Mack, who was getting higher by the minute, cracked a smile. "Yeah, well. It's the life, man. I ain't proud, but what the fuck you gonna do, right?"

"Look, Dennis, tell us what went on at Wonderland. What happened? Who would kill Mandy like that?" Drew had purposely used Mack's nickname for Amanda Quinn to make it personal. An important connection had to be made.

Mack sobbed intermittently, but he seemed to want to talk. He was a potential witness in a murder case and Drew would treat him as a witness regardless of his past until things changed. He had let Mack ingest the pills and hadn't admonished him over the use of drugs in his presence because he wanted the biker's cooperation.

Mack opened up more and told the detectives about staying at the house on Wonderland with Joe Allen, Harlan Tate, and the women. According to him, everyone at the house was doing drugs, and they were dealing out of the place. The biker then admitted they had been setting up robberies of other dope dealers in the Los Angeles area, taking down their competitors. They also had dealt in stolen property, including guns. Mack broke down in sobs at times. The drugs were doing a number on him. But the detectives had a witness they needed and weren't about to shut him down. Mack repeated again and again how much he had loved his girlfriend. Drew had set the hook and knew things were moving in the right direction. Now all he had to do was reel Mack in.

"Who do you think did the murders, Dennis?" he asked.

"I know exactly who did it," Mack said. "John fucking Watson and his Jamaican dude gangster buddy did the murders."

"The porn star?" Li asked. "That John Watson?" Drew made a note to self to ask Li later how she knew John Watson and that he was a porn star.

"Porn star, my ass. Porn punk, maybe," Mack said. Then he said that the porn actor, John Watson, had set up a robbery at the Studio City home of Tony Dunn, a local drug dealer, gangster, and the owner of a strip club on Sunset Boulevard. He stated further that he, Joe Allen, and Harlan Tate had ripped Dunn off for dope, money, and guns two days before the murders.

His outrage renewed by his telling of the story, Mack jumped to his feet once again. He had worked himself into a frenzy. He grabbed another pill from the table. "Christmas tree!" he shouted before popping it into his mouth. The man was frantic, but Drew didn't regard him as a threat to him or Li.

Li did a double take when Mack swallowed the pill and then glanced at Drew. He assumed Estrada had told her he was allowing Mack to pop pills during the interview, but maybe she hadn't believed it until seeing it with her own eyes. Drew looked back at her and shrugged. Mack had just given them some suspects with strong motives and he wouldn't take any action to stop the biker as long as he kept talking.

"Sit down, Dennis," Drew said. "Chill out, man." He tried his best to calm Mack down, knowing the man was coming apart rapidly from his despondence and the effects of the drugs. He continued taking notes while Mack ranted on, but became a little concerned when the man kept repeating to himself, "I don't give a shit!" Drew thought to himself that this could be good, or it could be bad.

Seated again at the table, the pill-popping biker suddenly opened up completely and provided the details Drew really wanted to hear.

Chapter Six

DENNIS MACK LAID OUT the Dunn robbery details for the detectives and told them more about the activities at the house on Wonderland Avenue that took place before the murders. However, the drugs he had taken were influencing his speech and thought process.

Among Mack's revelations was that the Dunn robbery getaway driver and lookout had been a guy named Bob Farmer, another Wonderland regular. Mack was clearly angry at John Watson and his shady antics.

"Watson must have rolled over on us to Dunn after the robbery," he said. "Then Dunn sent his posse to Wonderland to get payback and to get his property back."

Mack rattled on about Watson being terrified of Joe Allen and upset over him and Farmer only getting a small share of the booty from the Dunn robbery. Drew had Mack go over the details of the robbery a second time to check both his memory and veracity. He expected one day, Mack would testify in court. He would have to come across as credible to a jury, despite his checkered past.

The biker told the detectives he had Dunn and his bodyguard, a man named Justin Carr, on their knees and begging for their lives during the robbery after he had accidentally shot and grazed Carr with a bullet.

"I know it pissed off Joe, but it was his fault. He bumped into me and the damn gun went off."

Mack went on to say that it humiliated Dunn when they had forced him to open his safe and turn over his drugs and a large amount of cash, He also mentioned Joe Allen had wanted to kill Dunn, his bodyguard, and a young woman staying at the home at the time of the robbery, but he and Tate had talked him out of it.

"How did you guys get into Dunn's house with the bodyguard?" Drew asked.

"I used a stolen San Francisco police badge and convinced him we were cops," Mack said proudly. "We had used it before to gain entry for other drug rip-offs around LA."

It seemed to Drew that Mack didn't realize, or didn't care, the police badge ruse could tie him to other robberies and crimes, increasing his chances of arrest and eventual prison time. He always found it interesting that most armed robbers never seemed to realize the more robberies they committed, the greater the chance that the police would catch them because many crimes committed using the same MO naturally attracted more attention, manpower, and investigation.

Li left the room and returned with another cup of coffee for Mack. Then Drew told him to sit tight while he conferred with his partners outside the room. When he and Li stepped out into the hallway, Estrada was waiting, leaning against the wall with his arms crossed and a surly expression on his face. Drew could see he was still upset about the pill popping.

"Are we booking him?" Li asked, seemingly oblivious to Estrada's demeanor.

"How do you two think we should play it?" Drew asked. "I think if we book him on anything, he may feel betrayed and won't continue cooperating. I care more about solving our murder case than about some other drug dealer who may be one of our suspects getting robbed."

"If we kick him, he might get into the wind," Li said. "We might never see him again."

"I listened to the whole thing after leaving the room," Estrada said. "You need to consider another possibility. He's pissed about his girlfriend. He could go after Dunn and end up on a steel table at the coroner's office."

"Yeah, I agree it's a crapshoot," Drew said. "But his pal, Tiny Tim, needs a favor with the DA's office and we could hold his situation in abeyance if he agreed to play babysitter for Mack for a while."

"He has really jump-started our case," Li said. "I think kicking him is an acceptable risk, considering he might tell us to pound sand if he put charges on him and keep him locked up."

"After what went on in there, I'm not sure we can use him as a witness," Estrada said, eyeing Drew. "If some defense attorney gets wind of you letting him pop pills during that interview, he loses all credibility with any jury."

"That doesn't concern me," Drew said. "We didn't record this interview or videotape it. I think we can rehabilitate him as a witness by not mentioning this interview in the reports. We'll bring him in to the PAB in a couple of days and have him tell the complete story all over again on video when he is sober. Then we go with that."

"I will not lie if some defense attorney finds out about what went on here tonight and asks me about it," Estrada said testily. "You shouldn't have let that go down in there, Drew."

"It's water under the bridge now," Li said, acting as peacemaker. "I think we can massage the reports and he told the story once, so no reason he won't tell it again as long as he feels like we're treating him fairly."

Mack's future was in their hands, and Drew decided. He would kick Mack and they would play it out, keeping Tiny Tim on a tight leash.

Mack had passed out by the time the detectives reentered the interview room. Drew and Estrada roused him from his sleep and Drew gave him the usual admonishments about not leaving town and staying available after telling Mack they would not book him for forcing his way into a secured crime scene. Drew reiterated he expected to reach him with one call to Johnson. For what it was worth, Mack agreed.

The detectives escorted Mack out the back door of the station and turned him over to the care of Tim Johnson. Drew told Johnson that they would help make his situation with the DA's office go away as long as he kept Mack available to them and away from Tony Dunn. Johnson agreed, relieved that the detectives would not jail his friend.

Residing in the Cherokee Building, a historical landmark, was Boardner's, a neighborhood bar about a half mile from Hollywood Station. Drew and Li found themselves there some twenty minutes after Tim Johnson took off with Dennis Mack. Howard had invited his partners out for beers and burgers, intending it as a chance to catch their collective breaths and put their heads together while having a cold one or two and a late dinner. Drew considered such sessions good for morale and essential in working on their upcoming game plan. Estrada had begged off, saying his wife was holding dinner for him and he wasn't going home with alcohol on his breath. But Li had agreed to go.

When homicide detectives were officially off the clock and wrapping things up for a day, going straight home wasn't always the easiest thing to do. Complex cases had a way of hanging around twenty-four seven. If detectives didn't relax and brainstorm from time to time, they became much worse for the wear, physically and mentally. Drew had no one waiting for him at home anyway. He was seeing someone, Nina Garraway, but they didn't live together. He had been with Nina the day Moreno had phoned him on the callout.

"I don't think your tactics this evening impressed Oscar," Li said. "I'm used to you going outside policy sometimes to get results, Howie. But it looks like that rubs Oscar the wrong way. You better talk to him and try to mend fences."

"You think?" Drew said.

"Yes, we don't need an enemy inside the tent. He might already be Moreno's way of keeping a leash on you. He assigned Oscar to work with us."

Drew shrugged. "It's a big case, and we needed a third. I'm glad Moreno assigned someone without me having to ask. And Oscar seems competent."

"Still, we need to know he has our backs, Howie. Like you, I'm more concerned with getting results than following department policy chapter and paragraph. Still, you outdid yourself tonight letting that psycho pop pills during the interview."

"I don't disagree that it was a little over the top," Drew said. "But we got results. We now have solid suspects and solid motives just three days after the murders."

"So, what's the plan for tomorrow?" Li asked.

"In the morning, I'll put Oscar on a deep dive of Tony Dunn's background. Then you and I will drive up to Mount Olympus to interview the couple Tim Johnson mentioned this evening."

"Danny and Olivia Hatton?"

"Yeah, according to Tim, they frequently visited the house on Wonderland."

Once he started rambling under the influence of the drugs, Dennis Mack had mentioned in passing Danny Hatton and his wife Olivia being Wonderland frequent fliers, but had then gone off on another tangent. Drew hadn't known if it was important at the time. But when they walked Mack out to Johnson's Escalade, Drew had remembered the mention and asked Tim Johnson about the couple. Johnson had filled in a few blanks from Mack's interview and had seemed to know a lot of things about a lot of the people that had frequented Wonderland. Two of those people were Danny and Olivia Hatton. Danny Hatton was a singer-songwriter and the lead vocalist of a popular local rock band that had gone national.

"So, you want to talk to them mostly for background information?" Li asked.

"Yeah, and I just want to shake the tree and see what falls out."

Li nodded and drained the last swallow from her beer glass. "You sometimes get your best stuff that way, Howie."

Chapter Seven

GOING ON NINE O'CLOCK the following morning, Drew and Li pulled into the driveway of a large estate just off Laurel Canyon Boulevard in the Mount Olympus area of Los Angeles. As Drew drove in through the tall, decorative pilasters and up the winding drive, the detectives discovered the palatial entry was one thing. The grounds were another.

Approaching the main house, it was apparent the place needed a landscaper. The outward appearance of the house was no different. It was a large, ornate structure, probably built back in the nineteen twenties, and needed some serious care and a lot of paint. According to Tim Johnson, Danny and Olivia Hatton paid the rent on the Mount Olympus monstrosity.

Danny answered the door in a bathrobe. Drew and Li identified themselves, and he let them in. Hatton behaved as if he had been expecting the detectives and didn't question their presence. He appeared disheveled, and a little confused, like he might have had a hard night.

Oddly, Hatton turned his back to the detectives and placed his hands in the small of his back in the standard handcuffing position. Drew quickly explained they weren't there to arrest him and told him to relax.

Fidgeting with his robe, Hatton told them he would get dressed, but Drew told him not to bother. "We won't take up much of your time. We just have a few questions."

"Oh, this is about the thing in the canyon? I figured you guys would be by."

Danny's wife, Olivia, suddenly appeared and joined the trio in the foyer. Her appearance and demeanor differed little from her husband's. She also proved cooperative.

Following basic investigative technique, the detectives separated the couple and spoke with each separately to avoid one of them influencing the other's recollections. They would compare notes later and decide whether they would make a second visit. Drew stayed with Danny in the foyer and Li escorted Olivia to the kitchen.

Danny Hatton told Drew about how he had first met Nancy Poole three years earlier in West LA, just after her divorce. He said Nancy was his connection to the group up at Wonderland.

"I scored some lightweight shit at first. Later, me and Olivia scored blow and smack and whatever else we needed." Hatton shook his head as if in disbelief. "Christ, Olivia and I went through over a million bucks in smack in two years!"

Danny stated further that Nancy was a sweet lady who had the hots for him, and that had upset her boyfriend, Harlan Tate. He then related that once, while at Wonderland, he heard about a fat guy named Tim who fenced stolen property through Nancy and the others at the house. He had identified Timothy Johnson as the fence.

"Nancy was in way over her head, man. She didn't know how fast that crowd was."

As he talked, Drew saw Hatton became more relaxed, as if he was getting a load off his mind. He continued in his effusive manner, telling Drew about what he had seen and heard at the Wonderland house.

"Once this biker type, Dennis, came in with his girlfriend, Mandy, who I believe got killed at the house. I heard Dennis did burglaries with her. She was tiny and would crawl into houses through people's pet doors, then let Dennis inside to plunder."

Danny Hatton later said that he believed Nancy was the best thing that had ever happened to Harlan Tate.

"Harlan cleaned up his act for a while, but then started chipping again and before long he was back doing the hard stuff. Then Nancy got involved with the same hard drugs. Actually, the very night of the murders, Nancy called me, wanting us to come over and partake in what she said was a righteous score. But we had to decline because we were too sick." Drew understood Danny had meant drug sick.

"Do you know John Watson?" he asked.

"Yeah, the porn actor. He was a regular at Wonderland. He was always broke and scheming to scam some blow." Hatton elaborated, explaining that Watson was a wannabe and tried to act tough. "I saw Joe Allen slap him around on various occasions. They were trying to run their dope business like a legit undertaking and Watson was always bringing stolen shit into the house, radios, television sets, and even guns. Harlan got furious with Nancy once when he found out she had given Watson a key to the house."

Olivia was just as talkative as her husband and kept Li busy taking notes.

"This biker guy, Dennis, that hung out at the house kidnapped us once because we owed him money for some blow. But we got things straightened out quickly and he let us go. I don't think Dennis was a bad guy, but there was a psycho living there named Joe, who was mean and vicious."

Olivia Hatton closed out the interview with a jolt. She admitted that during the later morning hours of July first that she had gone to the Wonderland house and found the front door ajar.

"I stepped inside and saw Mandy Quinn on the floor beside the couch, covered with blood. I turned around and ran out of there."

"You didn't think about calling nine-one-one?" Li asked.

"I ran into a neighbor on the steps on the way out and told her what I had seen. I assumed she would call the police." But that hadn't happened.

By the end of the first week into the investigation, the workload was piling up. Tips and information on the victims and potential suspects came pouring in at a fast and furious pace. Drew and the team got some help from others in Homicide Special, but those detectives also had their own cases that needed their attention. Drew decided to split the team up temporarily and to divide the workload on the Laurel Canyon case. The coroner's office had scheduled the all important autopsies. It was critical for a member of the team to attend the postmortem exams. It was there that the homicide investigators would learn all about just who the victims were and how they died. With any luck, they might also glean evidence to those ends. Detectives learned what injuries were present and which had been fatal, as well as why the injuries had proved fatal. Autopsies were a critical evidentiary examination, and an investigator assigned to the case would have to attend every one of them.

Drew decided Oscar Estrada would stand the posts while Drew and Li attended all the other matters. Much of the information was time sensitive and required immediate attention.

Chapter Eight

ESTRADA ARRIVED AT the coroner's office and parked in the rear lot of the facility. The Los Angeles County Medical Examiner's Office, simply referred to as the coroner's office, was part of the sprawling Los Angeles County Hospital complex in nearby East Los Angeles. Estrada walked in through the rear entrance, where the attendants usually wheeled the bodies in. Entering the facility, it wasn't unusual to see one or two dozen bodies lined up in the corridor along the walls, sometimes two or three, on a gurney. This was especially true on weekends. The coroner's office was a twenty-four seven, three hundred and sixty-five days a year operation.

The detective met with pathologist Dr. Nina Garraway, a senior medical examiner. Having only recently met Howard Drew, he had no way of knowing that Drew and Garraway shared a romantic relationship. Garraway had expected Estrada as they had four examinations to perform that day. They got right to it.

Oscar Estrada did not particularly enjoy this part of his job as a homicide investigator, but he had no choice in the matter, and somehow that made it easier. Like most detectives who attended autopsies, the foul, nauseating odor of the specimen preservative mixed with the stench of decomposing human remains was the part he disliked most.

Gowned and attired in rubber gloves, a face shield, and protective footwear, throughout the lengthy procedure, Estrada took copious notes, asked many questions, and scrutinized a coroner's office photographer taking photos that memorialized all the facets of the examination. While doing so, Estrada also dodged the inadvertent splattering of human blood and tissues.

Standing in the main autopsies, Estrada saw other pathologists conducting autopsies nearby while he observed the ones performed by Dr. Garraway. It was a busy day for the "canoe makers", as homicide detectives often called the pathologists.

Assistants placed each body the pathologists would examine on a stainless-steel gurney with a six-inch curbing around its entire circumference to capture bodily fluids and other evidence. Prior to the examinations, the attendants had already washed down, weighed, measured, photographed, and toe-tagged the bodies. The photographs included close-ups of any visible wounds or infarctions to the body.

After Garraway finished the examinations, lab personnel would complete toxicology testing on all the victims, using their blood and tissue samples, screening for certain substances such as alcohol, poisons, and narcotics. Estrada knew it would be weeks before they completed the processing and provided reports.

Dr. Garraway noted needle marks, or tracks, some new and some old, on three of the four victims. She found none on Amanda Quinn. Joe Allen's right arm was abscessed because of drug injections. Harlan Tate had many needle marks on the insides of his arms, most somewhat obscured by tattoos. Estrada knew junkies often took extreme measures to conceal needle tracks.

The pathologist noted the injuries sustained by all four victims had resulted from repeated blows to the head with blunt objects. Nancy Poole had sustained the worst injuries, her head battered flat from the eyebrows back. Harlan Tate was the only victim with defensive wounds. Estrada recalled from his crime scene observations that Tate had fought back against his attackers to some extent. Garraway noted some of his fingers and ribs had suffered fractures, injuries he sustained while trying to defend himself from his assailants.

Dr. Garraway cut a Y incision into the thorax region of each victim using a scalpel, beginning at the top of each shoulder and slicing downward at an approximate forty-five-degree angle across the chest toward the navel where the twin incisions met. She separated the large flap of flesh, forming the chest area with the scalpel, and peeled it back over the face and head, exposing the rib cage. Her assistant cut out the entire rib cage using a tool resembling a garden trimmer with two- or three-inch crescent shaped blades.

Using the scalpel, the pathologist then removed the internal organs from the thorax region for cross sectioning. This created the "canoe" effect that caused detectives to call pathologists canoe makers. She sliced open the stomach of each victim and examined them thoroughly for contents. Stomach contents from a last meal because of the digestive process often helped determine the time of death.

Finished with the thorax area, Dr. Garraway turned her attention to the head of each of the victims, propped on wooden blocks. She made an incision with the scalpel roughly from ear to ear, slicing the scalp around the back of the head, and then pulled the scalp forward and down over the face of each body, exposing the skull. Using a small handheld circular power saw, her assistant then cut through the skull, moving the saw around the entire circumference of the cranium. After the sawing, the assistant pried off the skullcap with a tool and removed it, exposing the brain.

The condition of the skulls of these victims, bashed repeatedly with a blunt instrument, made this part somewhat of a challenge. Mostly, all the skulls had cracks and shattered portions and striation marks existed in some portions of the skulls. Dr. Garraway noted many of the wounds showed the characteristics of the threaded end portion of a length of metal pipe measuring three-quarters to one and one-half inches in diameter.

After completing the examination of each body, the pathologist and her assistant bagged all the organs and placed the plastic bags back into the chest cavities, which Dr. Garraway stitched closed with heavy twine.

The autopsies complete, Estrada spoke with Dr. Garraway before returning to the PAB to rejoin Drew and Li. It didn't surprise him when the pathologist told him all four victims died from blunt-force trauma and extensive brain damage. She also told him she believed it would be beneficial for her to examine Dawn Allen and her wounds, dead or alive, for evidentiary comparative purposes. Estrada agreed to speak with the neurologist treating Allen to coordinate Garraway's examination at Cedars-Sinai. He then left the coroner's office, heading back downtown to the PAB.

Chapter Nine

THE DAY AFTER THE AUTOPSIES, Drew was at his desk, putting more information together on the four victims. Amy Li, at her desk beside him, was taking calls screened by other detectives in the office that sounded productive. Estrada was on his way to Cedars-Sinai Hospital to meet with Dr. Garraway, the pathologist and Dr. Marc Cohen, the neurologist heading up Dawn Allen's treatment to discuss her condition and to facilitate Dr. Garraway's examination and comparison of Allen's wounds with those of the four deceased victims.

Delving into the past histories of the Wonderland victims, it was clear to Howard Drew that the number one badass was Joe Allen. Homicide Special detectives Richard Lewis and Jeff Eldridge had given Drew more information regarding Allen's suspected involvement in the killing of Los Angeles sports promoter Albert Stern. The detectives had an informant who had told them that Allen had shown up at Stern's Long Beach home to pick him up and take him to a party. Two days later, police officers had found Stern shot dead in the trunk of his vehicle. If the informant's story was true, that meant Joe Allen might have been the last person to see Stern alive. While Lewis and Eldridge would continue their investigation of the Stern murder, that scenario left them with more questions than answers.

Drew had also learned Allen had had a court date in Sacramento on July second, on drug charges. He had spoken to a detective at the Yuba County Sheriff's Office about Allen. The detective, who had known Allen for several years, had stated sarcastically that the death of Joe Allen was "a real loss to the greater community of criminals, and an act of poetic justice." The same detective had also told Drew that Allen had received a bad conduct discharge from the U.S. Army. He had also related that Allen had been involved in several drug heists and other robberies and possibly a murder for hire in the Sacramento area.

Harlan Tate, Drew discovered, had a criminal record dating back to the late nineteen nineties that included robbery, assault, burglary, drugs, and drunk driving. His estranged wife and daughter lived in the San Gabriel Valley. Tate had also had an adult son who was in the U.S. Air Force. His criminal record aside, it appeared Tate had at least for a time been a family man. He had worked in construction for over twenty years. Los Angeles area undercover narcotics officers had made a few buys from Tate and he had one local drug case pending.

In a recorded telephone interview the previous day with Tate's adult son, William Tate had told Drew that his father had had problems with alcohol while working in the oilfield and had stated his father had always seemed in the middle of trouble or chasing trouble. William also told Drew his dad had once been "good buddies" with a man named Jack Langley, who had been into "some nasty shit."

Nancy Poole turned out something of a paradoxical figure to Drew. She had once been married to a successful Westside attorney and was the mother of two daughters. It seemed Poole's life had taken a dramatic turn for the worse after doctors diagnosed her with cancer and she had undergone a double mastectomy. After her divorce, she became involved with Harlan Tate and that was when her criminal record began—three drug arrests and one arrest for drunk driving.

Drew found that Amanda Quinn had come from a solid, suburban working-class family in Sacramento. She had no criminal record and her family had known little about her much older boyfriend, Dennis Mack. She had hooked up with Mack after a brief marriage. Her murder had decimated her parents, who would forever be haunted by the unspeakable crime committed against their daughter. Drew felt convinced Amanda Quinn had died simply because she had been in the wrong place at the worst possible time. He didn't know how Quinn had come to be at the Wonderland House overnight while her boyfriend, Dennis Mack, hadn't been and made a note to ask Mack about it when he next talked with the man.

During the investigation, as with every murder he had investigated, Drew had turned to the field interview card database maintained by the LAPD Records and Identification Division, which often proved to be a key source of information. Primarily, patrol officers completed the field interview cards, referred to as "shakes", following some type of field interaction with citizens. A check of the database by Drew had revealed a contact with Jack Langley and a girlfriend, Megan Dixon. The officer completing the shake card had associated them with Mack's pal, Tiny Tim Johnson, and this made Drew interested in interviewing them.

Drew had run the names through the criss-cross directory on his computer but wasn't able to find a current address or phone number for Langley. But he found a number for Megan Dixon assigned to an address in the Burbank area, just northeast of Los Angeles. He figured she might know where he could find Langley. He rolled his chair back to look at Li around the cubicle divider that separated their desks.

"Want to get out of the office for a while, Amy?" he asked.

"Sure, what's up?" Li answered, still looking at her computer screen with her fingers flying over the keyboard in front of her.

"I found a couple of names from a shake card," Drew said. "I want to interview the guy, but can't find a current address or phone number. But I found a Burbank address for his girlfriend and I want to make a run over there."

"Okay," Li said, shutting down her computer. "Let's do it and then we can grab lunch before we come back here afterward."

Li pulled into the parking lot of a small apartment building made of wood and stucco on Peyton Avenue in Burbank. The detectives got out and took the stairs up to the second-floor apartment listed in the address Drew had found in the criss-cross directory. Apartment dwellers often moved frequently, so Drew knew it was a long shot that Dixon still lived at the address. But he had wanted a break from the office and the tedious paperwork for a while and it was almost time for lunch anyway, so he figured it was worth the twenty-five-minute drive to Burbank. He hadn't called first because he hadn't wanted to tip off Dixon that they were coming to see her.

Drew knocked on the door. A few moments later, a brunette who looked like late thirties wearing a T-shirt and yoga pants opened the door.

"Can I help you?" she said.

"I'm Detective Drew, LAPD," Drew said, holding up his badge case. "This is Detective Li, my partner. You're Megan Dixon?"

"That's right. What's this about?"

"We would appreciate a few minutes of your time, Ms. Dixon. May we come in?"

"Is this about Jack? I'm not seeing him anymore."

"If you mean Jack Langley, yes, we have some questions about him. But we wanted to ask you a few other questions as well. We're investigating a murder case where four people got killed a week ago in Laurel Canyon."

"The Wonderland murders? Yes, I saw that on the news. But what does it have to do with me?"

"Nothing, I'm sure," Drew said. "Mind if we talk inside?"

"All right, sure," Dixon said, stepping back to allow the detectives to enter. She directed them to the living room. Drew and Li sat down on a sofa, and Dixon took a chair across from them.

"Do you suspect Jack was involved in the murders? Because if you do, I doubt I can tell you anything useful. We broke up months ago and I haven't heard from Jack in weeks."

"He isn't a suspect, but his name came up in an interview with another witness in connection with people visiting the house regularly where the murders occurred. Do you know someone named Timothy Johnson?"

Dixon's brow furrowed, as if she were thinking. "I don't think so. The name doesn't ring any bells."

"A tall, heavyset guy who goes by the nickname Tiny Tim."

"Oh, him. Yes, I know who that is. I don't believe I ever heard his last name. Jack knew him and I only know who he is because of Jack."

"Did you know any of the murder victims?"

"I knew who some of them were, but didn't really know them. Again, I only know about them because of Jack."

"So, he knew the people who lived in the house?"

"Yes, he was good friends with Harlan Tate. I think they used to work with each other before I met Jack."

"Was Jack friends with Joe Allen?"

"Hardly. I remember Jack saying once he was going to kill Joe Allen. He not only threatened to kill him, but others living in that house."

Drew raised his eyebrows. "When did he say that?"

"The last time I saw Jack, maybe two weeks ago. I was at a club with a girlfriend and Jack came in. He saw me and came over and we spoke for a few minutes. He was angry at some people living there over some type of business arrangement, but he didn't tell me any of the details."

"You think Jack could have killed those people?"

"Is Jack capable of murdering someone? Yes, I believe he is if he thought he had a good reason. But I have no reason to believe he did it and do not know when he was last at that house."

"What makes you say you believe Jack is capable of murder if he thought he had a good reason?"

"Jack has a temper and can be violent. I knew he was the bad boy type when I met him. Honestly, I'm ashamed to admit it, but that was part of the attraction for me at the time. But I just didn't know how bad he really was. As soon as I realized it, I ended things with him and cut my losses, you know? Jack Langley is a dangerous man."

"You know how we can get in touch with Jack?" Drew asked. "We haven't been able to find a current address or telephone number for him."

Dixon shook her head. "I don't have his number and I don't know where he is living now. But you could probably find out from Tim. They are good friends and I know they were still hanging out when we broke up. I assume they still are."

Drew and Li thanked Dixon for her time and left the apartment.

"You think Langley is a solid suspect?" Li asked after they got back in her city ride.

"Well, I'm not tunneling in on him, but based on what Dennis Mack told us, I still like Tony Dunn for the murders. But I'm not ruling Langley out for one reason, after talking to his ex-girlfriend."

"What's the reason?"

"If there is a trial, some smart defense attorney will probably find out somehow that Langley threatened to kill Allen and others at the Wonderland House. And they would put Langley out front as the number one suspect in an alternative perpetrator defense to create reasonable doubt. We need to knock that down preemptively by excluding Langley as a suspect ourselves."

"Assuming he didn't do it," Li said.

"Yeah, there is that," Drew agreed, taking out his phone. He called Tim Johnson. Johnson picked up on the third ring.

"Talk to me."

"Tim, this is Detective Drew."

"I've got it under control, Detective. I'm keeping Denny out of trouble, just like you said."

"That's terrific, Tim, but I want to ask you about someone else. Tell me about Jack Langley."

Johnson's demeanor changed immediately. He dodged Drew's questions and became cagey and even snarky when Drew pressed him for answers.

"Listen, Tim. The more I'm learning about you, the more I think the minor misdemeanor beef you want us to help you with is the least of your worries. I think I could put you in prison for a long time. Now, stop fucking around and tell me about Jack Langley."

Johnson's telephone demeanor quickly improved. "What do you want to know?"

"Where to find him. We need to talk to him. A witness told us he recently threatened to kill Joe Allen and some of the other people living at the Wonderland House."

"You're putting me in a tough position, Detective. Jack is a friend, and he is also dangerous. How about if I arrange a meeting for you instead of rolling over on him by giving up his address?"

"That works as long as you deliver, Tim," Drew said. "Tell him we aren't looking at him as a suspect. But since someone told us about the threats, we have to exclude him. And it would go a long way towards proving his innocence to us if he voluntarily comes in and makes a statement. If we have to find him, which we will if it comes to that, we will be a lot harder to convince."

"Okay, I'll set it up and then I'll call you back, Detective."

"Call me soon, Tim. Soon." Drew ended the call.

"Tiny Tim is becoming as much a find as Mack," Li said.

"Yeah, he's turning into a regular CI. Now let's get some lunch."

Chapter Ten

ABOUT AN HOUR AFTER they got back to the PAB, Drew received a telephone call from Lieutenant Chris Greer with the Los Angeles County Sheriff's Department Narcotics Bureau. He told Drew one of their informants had recently bought cocaine at the home of Tony Dunn in Studio City. The narcotics bureau had obtained a search warrant for the residence because of that buy. The sheriff's department viewed Dunn as a major narcotics distributor in the Los Angeles area. Having knowledge of the recent savage murders on Wonderland Avenue and LAPD's interest in Dunn as a suspect, Greer asked Drew if his team of detectives would care to accompany his deputies when they served the warrant the following Friday morning. Drew jumped at the opportunity and Greer briefed him on the where and when details.

Oscar Estrada had returned to the PAB and had briefed Drew and Li on the pathologist's examination of Dawn Allen at Cedars-Sinai Hospital. Dr. Garraway had found conclusive evidence that Dawn Allen had sustained the same type injuries as the four deceased victims she had autopsied including impressions from the threaded end of a steel pipe. Estrada also reported that Allen remained unconscious and unavailable for interview.

Minutes after Estrada completed his briefing, Tim Johnson called Drew and told him he had convinced a reluctant Jack Langley to come to police headquarters for an interview and told Drew that Langley was on his way there. Drew asked Johnson if Dennis Mack was sober and when Johnson assured him he was, Drew told him to bring Mack to the PAB for an official interview. When Johnson objected, saying he didn't think it was a good idea for Langley and Mack to both appear at police headquarters at the same time, Drew assured him they would keep them separated and neither man would know the other was there. Johnson reluctantly agreed and told Drew he would bring Mack to the PAB within the hour. Drew called his partners together for a meeting.

"We have Langley on his way here for an interview," Drew said, after bringing Estrada up to speed on Jack Langley. "And I told Johnson to bring Mack in for an official videotaped interview. We have to keep them separated, so we need to divide the workload again."

Estrada spoke up quickly. "I can take Langley," he said. "You and Amy can handle Mack. You interviewed him at Hollywood Station and already established a rapport."

Drew could see that Estrada still had a problem with the first interview of Mack at Hollywood Station. He had already expressed his belief that Mack was tainted and no longer useful as a witness, and if the pill-popping story came to light, it would not only destroy Mack's credibility, but that of the entire investigative team. Drew didn't agree, but he respected Estrada's opinion and was happy to go along with his suggestion.

"Okay, you take Langley and Amy and I will take Mack," Drew said. Then he told Estrada and Li about the LASD warrant raid they would take part in early Friday morning.

When Jack Langley arrived in the lobby, Estrada went downstairs to escort him up to the fifth floor. Then he ushered Langley into an interview room. Quickly, Estrada got the message that Langley didn't want to talk to a homicide cop investigating a quadruple murder. But he also didn't want to be a suspect, and agreed to answer questions.

"We talked to someone who told us you threatened to kill Joe Allen and others at the house on Wonderland," Estrada said.

"It wasn't me, man. You know how it is, right? I was angry about a business deal. Allen didn't deliver on his end, and I got angry. Yeah, I might have told someone I was going to kill him and Tate. But I didn't mean it. I was just angry, you know?"

"Easy way you can get out from under it," Estrada said. "You only need to give me an alibi covering one to five o'clock, the morning of July second. An alibi we can confirm when we check, and believe me, we will check."

"Sure, no problem. I can do that. I was nowhere near the house when that shit went down."

Langley came up with a fairly decent alibi. Estrada took out his cell phone and stepped outside the room to call the number for the person Langley had told him would back up his story. He spoke with a woman named Daisy Gilbert. She told him she lived in Las Vegas and that Jack Langley had visited her there, arriving the twenty-eighth of June and had stayed until the morning of July fifth when he had left to return to LA.

Gilbert said they visited several of the casinos, one she worked at, and she knew they all kept their CCTV camera recordings for thirty days. Gilbert told him she was certain that if he checked with the security offices at the casinos, he would find footage showing both her and Jack if he wanted to verify her story. Then she gave him a list of the casinos they had gambling at. Estrada intended to do that, but he had found Gilbert credible.

Jack Langley had known the victims and also knew Dennis Mack. Estrada didn't doubt the nature of his business dealings up at Wonderland. He had dealt with many bad guys over the years and recognized Langley was one of the nastier ones. But the vibes weren't there when he had talked with Langley, and the alibi seemed solid. Estrada felt satisfied Langley hadn't been involved in the murders and there was no evidence he was. As far as the LAPD was concerned, Jack Langley was not a suspect.

After checking to make sure Dennis Mack was in an interview room with Drew and Li and finding he was, Estrada went back into the room with Langley. He told him the alibi checked out and thanked him for coming in. Then he escorted Langley back downstairs to the lobby and sent him on his way.

When Dennis Mack arrived, he was sober, as Tim Johnson had asserted. Drew and Li took him back to an interview room. Before they started recording, Drew had considered telling Mack outright not to mention the previous interview at Hollywood Station and to just forget it ever happened. But he wasn't prepared to actually do anything unlawful or give the appearance he was manipulating the testimony of a witness. So, instead, he explained to Mack that they were interviewing him again because he had been upset and high when they had talked to him the first time. He reminded Mack he would need to appear credible if there was a trial. Given his checkered past, they didn't need his testimony tainted by emotional distress and pill popping. So, they wanted a clean interview they would record and would ask him the same questions again. Mack agreed and seemed relaxed.

Drew felt relief once they completed the interview. He hadn't mentioned the first interview, and neither had Mack. And Mack had been just as forthcoming and even more persuasive while sober. He had again implicated Tony Dunn, asserting Dunn had orchestrated the murders at the house on Wonderland Avenue in vengeance because he, Allen, and Tate had robbed Dunn's Studio City house two days earlier.

As Mack recounted the Dunn robbery, Drew asked him if they had targeted Dunn for the same reason as the other drug dealers they had robbed. Mack said no, they had done a lot of business with Dunn previously, but Joe Allen had a falling out with Dunn over some guns Dunn had agreed to sell for him. Dunn took them, but whenever Allen had asked when he would get the money, Dunn kept making excuses, telling Allen the guns were too expensive and he had found no one willing to pay what they were worth. After a couple of weeks went by, Allen told Dunn to forget it and to return the guns, but again Dunn kept stalling. Mack said they had gone to Dunn's house only to take the guns back, but once they got inside, they found only a few of the guns and knew Dunn had sold the bulk of them and kept the money. That was when Allen decided to take Dunn's dope and money.

After they finished the interview and Li had stopped the recording and left the room, Drew asked Mack one last question.

"There is one other question I want to ask you," Drew said.

"Sure, man," Mack said. "I'm an open book. Ask."

"Where were you when the murders happened? Mandy was spending the night at the house. Why weren't you there?"

Mack's face flushed immediately, and for the first time during the interview, Drew saw he was uncomfortable.

"Sorry, but I have to ask," Drew explained. "If there is a trial, the lawyers will ask the question. Defense attorneys might try to put you out there as a suspect, saying you weren't there because you knew what was going to happen. I don't believe that. But I think you can see where I'm coming from."

"I was partying with a friend at a motel up in the San Fernando Valley. I loved Mandy. There is no way I would have left her at the house if I'd known what was going down, man."

"Another woman?" Drew asked. "The friend you partied with."

"No, man. Just a dude, a friend, you know? I just like partying with him sometimes. Especially when I'm feeling stressed. And I was feeling it because I was worried about us robbing Dunn. I never thought that was smart, and I had tried to talk Joe out of it. But he wouldn't listen. I never expected Dunn to kill everyone, but I expected Dunn would be after payback."

"What's the friend's name?" Drew asked.

"Come on, man. I don't want to drag him into this. He isn't part of it."

"We need to verify you have a solid alibi," Drew said. "That's why we need the name. If there is a trial, we have to show we looked at every potential suspect and that we eliminated you."

Mack sighed. "Curt. Curtis Tomlinson."

"How did you make his acquaintance? You know him from somewhere?"

"No, man. We met at a bar on Santa Monica in West Hollywood one time after I moved down from Sacto. We hit it off and we get together to party sometimes. That's it."

"You got his number?"

Mack sighed again, clearly uncomfortable. He took out his phone, thumbed through the contacts, and read off a phone number that Drew copied down.

"Is that it?" Mack asked. "Can I get out of here?"

"Yes, that's all for now," Drew said, standing. "Come on, I'll walk you out. Thanks for coming in."

Mack's demeanor had sparked Drew's curiosity. He hadn't been comfortable at all discussing Tomlinson, and Drew intended to find out why.

Chapter Eleven

IT WAS FOUR O'CLOCK Friday morning when Drew, Li, and Estrada rolled up on the field command post that LASD had established a few blocks down the hill from Dunn's Studio City home. The detectives met with their sheriff's department counterparts and Los Angeles County Deputy District Attorney Alex Douglas, who had assisted the sheriff's department with writing the so-called "no-knock" warrant. Also present was the Los Angeles County Sheriff's elite Special Enforcement Bureau (SEB), the equivalent of the LAPD's SWAT unit.

The SEB commander outlined the plan to hit the house just as dawn broke. Twenty SEB deputies would approach on foot, surround the house, and await the signal to make entry. The signal for the other deputies would be the detonation of a flash-bang inside the house by the front door entry team after they rammed the door. When it happened, the remaining members of SEB would force entry at their assigned points around the perimeter of the house. Wearing body armor, the heavily armed deputies would confront whoever they found inside. The Homicide Special detectives and the deputy DA would wait at the command post until SEB notified them they had secured the house.

Just as the sun broke over the hills to the east, the detectives heard a thunderous explosion that disrupted the peace of the entire neighborhood. Within seconds of the blast, they heard glass breaking, shouted commands, three rapid gunshots, and what sounded like two shotgun blasts. Then silence reigned.

The SEB commander reported to the command post that an entry team had taken gunfire from inside the house on the east side of the property. Ten minutes later, he gave the all clear signal and the LAPD detectives and deputy DA started uphill behind several squad cars and SEB tactical vehicles. As they approached the front of the house, they saw several law enforcement officers moving in and out of the house, along with the narcotics unit deputies with the warrant.

Drew, Li, and Estrada entered through the foyer and found the inside of the house in a shambles. The deputies had forcibly entered from six separate points. Besides broken windows and broken sliding glass doors, there was overturned furniture throughout. Narcotics unit deputies searched drawers and closets, tossing the contents into the center of the rooms.

In the middle of a downstairs room, the detectives observed a muscular black man lying nude on his stomach on a pool table with his hands handcuffed behind his back. A SEB deputy told Drew the man was Dunn's bodyguard, Justin Carr. Drew had heard the name before from Dennis Mack. One entry point on the east side of the house had been the bedroom Carr had been sleeping in. When the deputies broke the glass and roused him, Carr had grabbed a handgun and opened fire on the deputies. The deputies had returned fire with shotguns, but miraculously, no one got hit in the exchange of gunfire. Carr was lucky to be alive. Drew wondered if the man had thought it was another robbery when he woke up.

The SEB deputy escorted the detectives to the rear of the living room, where they saw Tony Dunn seated in a chair and handcuffed. Dunn was a gaunt looking black man with a perfectly shaven head in his late forties. His face was a mixture of dismay and anger as he surveyed his ruined home. Disheveled did not begin to describe his appearance.

"Why do you guys fuck with me?" Dunn snarled in a Jamaican accent. "Why? I'm not the only guy in LA with coke in my house? I'm a friend of the police."

Two LASD narcotics unit deputies helped Dunn to his feet and explained they wanted him to open his safe in the bedroom closet. They led him in that direction, and the LAPD detectives followed. Once inside the bedroom, the deputies removed his handcuffs and Dunn complied. After he entered the combination and opened the safe door, the other deputies pulled him aside. The narcotics unit officers began pulling guns, cash, and a large stash of bagged powdered cocaine out of the safe.

As deputies put the handcuffs back on him, Dunn again complained.

"Why me? Why are you doing this?"

Drew glanced over at Dunn's unmade bed. Stuffed clumsily beneath the bed were reams of papers and documents. His curiosity piqued, Drew walked to the bed, bent down, and pulled out the papers. He quickly realized the stash contained legal documents, police reports, law enforcement intelligence sheets, copies of warrants, and even warrant affidavits. Warning bells rang. The affidavit portion of a warrant describes details of an investigation that only a judge and those involved in an investigation should know. Often the affidavits contain witness information and confidential informant disclosures, critical information in any investigation.

Drew found it alarming that the affidavits in Dunn's possession named several people and, among the documents, he also found confidential LAPD intelligence reports. It seemed obvious that Dunn had someone, perhaps several people at the LAPD, on his payroll, supplying him with sensitive law enforcement information.

The Homicide Special detectives arrived at their fifth-floor office two hours after the LASD warrant raid had started. Drew had taken custody of all the documents he had found in Dunn's bedroom. He left Li and Estrada at their desks, inventorying and cataloging the papers and documents to prepare for booking them into property and sending a list to the LASD narcotics unit to include with their warrant return. Drew went directly to Lieutenant Moreno's office to brief him on the raid of Dunn's home and to tell him what he had found there. He had three representative documents with him.

Drew found Moreno at his desk, reviewing his morning reports. He knocked lightly on the door frame and then walked through the open doorway.

"How did it go?" Moreno asked, referring to the raid. Drew had already told him that he and his team were accompanying LASD on the warrant service.

"LASD recovered guns, cash, and a substantial stash of cocaine," Drew said. "But I found something troubling in Dunn's bedroom." He laid the three documents on the lieutenant's desk. Moreno picked them up and scanned them.

"What the hell?" Moreno exclaimed. "Warrant affidavits, intel reports!"

"Looks like Dunn has someone inside the department on his payroll, Lieutenant," Drew said. "No other explanation for how he came into possession of these documents. And I brought back an armload. Li and Estrada are inventorying and cataloging them now."

"Christ. This means anther internal investigation, another scandal, and another black eye for the LAPD."

"There is no way of knowing what all is getting sent to Dunn. I'm worried about my investigation getting compromised."

"I'll talk to the captain as soon as we finish here," Moreno said. "For now, I want nothing in your investigation concerning Dunn put on the system. Document it with manual murder book entries for now until we identify and plug the leak."

"Yes, Sir."

"Anything else, Drew?"

"Yes, it's still early in the investigation, but I think we need to talk to Tony Dunn."

"You think it wise to tip him he's a suspect this early in the game? And who's to say he will talk to you anyway? He may just lawyer up."

"We've already mentioned his name in reports Li has put on the system. After what I found out this morning, he may already know we're looking at him. Dunn is clearly a narcissistic sort with violent tendencies. I think we need to hit him in the mouth, so to speak, just to let him know he doesn't intimidate the cops. I think if we attack his sensitive ego, he might say something stupid we can use. And we won't know unless we make the attempt. It looks like Dunn has well insulated himself over the years and knows many influential people. From what I discovered this morning, some may be cops."

"I don't think we have enough to go hard at him yet," Moreno said, revealing his skepticism. "And before we do that, I want to speak to the captain about it first."

"Can we ask him?" Drew said. "Everyone wants a quick resolution. I'm confident we can break him with an interrogation."

Moreno ran a hand over his silvery gray hair. Then he stood up. "Wait here, Detective. I'll go ask him." Then Moreno left the office.

Moreno was in and out of the captain's office so quickly, Drew hadn't even had time to sit down to wait.

"Don't talk to Tony Dunn. Not yet, and never, without clearing it with me first."

"Yes, Sir," Drew said, not bothering to hide his disappointment. "Then I'll get back to work."

On his way back to his desk, Drew felt the anger rising from his gut. The brass had always allowed Homicide Special detectives to function with near-complete autonomy in their investigations. All the bosses cared about were results that made them look good. Why the roadblock? The time to get Dunn was now, not later, while he was reeling from the aftermath of the LASD raid this morning. Why would Captain Meyer nix the idea, and so quickly?

Chapter Twelve

SITTING AT HIS DESK, Drew continued mulling over Captain Meyers' immediate decision to deny him permission to interview Tony Dunn. Drew had heard rumors about LAPD detectives frequenting Dunn's clubs, the Fiction on Sunset Boulevard in particular. According to the rumors, cops who ate and drank there never paid the cover charge and never received a bill. The custom seemed to be to leave only a minimal tip for the server. Drew wondered if that had been what Dunn meant when he claimed to be "a friend of the police." He knew that restaurant and bar owners who comped checks and tabs for cops always expected some favor in return, even if it was something as innocuous as overlooking a code violation or fixing a traffic ticket. Drew wondered now how many cops in the LAPD owed favors to Tony Dunn and just how high up the chain Dunn's "friends" in the department went.

Drew didn't know Captain William Meyers well. The chief of police had chosen him to be the commanding officer of the Robbery-Homicide Division when Captain Kenneth Mann had retired under a cloud. Meyers raised no particular feelings for Drew. He was a tall, distinguished looking man who wouldn't get caught with a hair out of place, much less his shoes not shined. Meyers was the aloof type who carried himself with an air of vanity. He would never leave his office without his jacket on and buttoned. He didn't socialize with the troops after hours. Meyers engendered little loyalty among the members of RHD, but he created little enmity. Drew wasn't ready to accept the man was in Dunn's pocket, but he was certainly going to keep his eyes open. Of course, Drew allowed it might not be corruption, but politics that was at fault.

Certainly, the quadruple murder case drew a tremendous amount of scrutiny. Maybe the brass upstairs was more concerned with the department's public facing image than with a quick and successful resolution of the case. Maybe they worried investigators might appear overbearing or the public might consider their efforts untoward for some reason. All Drew knew was it wasn't a time for tiptoeing when someone had brutally slaughtered those four people up in Laurel Canyon and left a fifth victim barely clinging to life.

With the hands-off warning on Tony Dunn, Drew saw continuing to work the investigation as the only path forward. Maybe they would find out more about Dunn, enough to convince Captain Meyers of his guilt to get him to remove the roadblock. While planning his next move, Drew's desk phone rang.

"Detective Drew."

"Detective, this is Dennis Mack."

"What can I do for you, Dennis?"

"You asked me how you could get in touch with Bob Farmer."

"Yeah?"

"He just called me from Bauchet to see if I'd help him raise bail. He's in on a felony theft charge."

Drew knew Bauchet was the term used by cops and hooks alike for Men's Central Jail on Bauchet Street.

"Thanks for the tip, Dennis. We'll go over and talk to Bob."

Drew hung up, thinking Mack might be a bad dude, but so far, he had been a straight shooter.

After checking with Lin and Estrada, Drew left Lin at the office to catch up on reports and took Estrada with him to Bauchet.

When a jailer brought Bob Farmer into the interview room, Drew could tell with one look Farmer was the kind of guy you wouldn't trust with a copy of last week's newspaper. He was a mousy looking, skinny hype who obviously couldn't keep his grubby hands off other people's property. It surprised Drew that Farmer appeared happy to see him and Estrada. Apparently, he didn't get many visitors and was happy to see anyone. Drew intended to change that in a hurry.

Drew and Estrada had discussed it on the drive over. They would first probe Farmer with a little "acid test" to see if he would give them anything of relevance. They didn't want to alienate him because they knew they might need him down the road if there was a trial. Although Drew didn't tolerate bullshit from those he interviewed, he still treated people like Farmer with a modicum of respect, whether they deserved it or not. And Drew figured a guy like Farmer would be vulnerable to the simple strategy of good cop/bad cop. Drew would be the good cop and Estrada would play the bad cop. Drew knew most seasoned detectives could sell it with a little acting work.

"Bob, we want to know everything you know about the goings on up at Wonderland," Drew said, bracing Farmer right out of the gate to let him know they were there for a serious discussion of a serious matter.

"Wonderland? I know nothing about it. I don't even know where it is."

Estrada got right in Farmer's face. "Hey, Bob. Do we look stupid to you?" Estrada hovered over the frightened addict and appeared pissed off.

Drew took over, using a moderately conciliatory tone. "Bob, we know better. Help us out here. It will go so much better for you in the long run."

Tears welled in Farmer's eyes and he started blubbering about getting people killed.

"Look, I wasn't there when it happened. I scored some drugs there in the past and Joe was a pretty good dude when he wasn't being a hard-ass. But I know nothing about the murders. I swear it."

Farmer's offer of general information would not cut it with the detectives, and Drew changed tack.

"What about the Dunn robbery?" Drew asked. "You were in on it, weren't you?"

Drew and Estrada already knew the answer, but it had to come from Farmer.

"I know nothing about any robbery. I'm a thief, but I don't rob people."

Estrada got in Farmer's face again. "Hey, shit bird. If you're going to lie to us, lie to us about shit we don't know already."

Farmer's tears and blubbering started again. He was a weak and unconvincing liar.

After a few more disgusted glances and a little more intimidation from Estrada, Farmer recounted his role in the Dunn robbery.

"I drove the car," Farmer admitted. "A piece of shit Corolla. But I didn't know that Joe had stolen it until later. And when we got there, I was the lookout. That's all I had to do with it, man. I swear."

"You stayed in the car the entire time?" Drew asked.

"Yes, and it stressed me out. They were inside forever."

"Then what happened, Bob?"

"They came out with all kinds of guns wrapped in a shower curtain. Harlan stopped a couple of times to pick up shit they dropped. And he had so much cash stuffed in his pockets, it fell out while he was running to the car."

As he continued the story, Farmer picked up the pace.

"Joe got pissed at Dennis because he shot some black guy in the back, Dunn's bodyguard."

"Who is Dennis?" Drew asked, running cover for Mack so Farmer wouldn't know he had tipped them that Farmer was in custody. "What do you know about him?"

"Dennis Mack. He's a biker dude and was part of the regular crew. Joe brought him down from Sacramento to help with the business. They did time together in Chino."

"Who handled the gang's stolen property?" Drew asked.

"A fence up in Laurel Canyon by the name of Chelo is the only guy I know about."

"You got a last name?" Drew asked.

"No, Chelo is the only name I ever heard. He lives in the Hollywood Hills somewhere above Wonderland and I know he fenced loads of property for Joe and his crew and for other people."

"Tell us what you know about the murders, Bob. The people you were running with, you have to know something or heard something after the murders. Who do you think did it?"

"I swear it, you guys. I seriously know nothing about it. Some people went up to the house right after to score dope before the cops showed up. That's what some people I know told me. But that's all I know."

"Give us names, Bob," Drew said. "Who went up there?"

"I don't have any names. I swear."

"You got to do better than that, asshole," Estrada seethed, getting back in Farmer's grill. Farmer appeared more and more frightened of Estrada.

"Okay, okay," Farmer said. "Let's see, there was a guy by the name of Stretch and one called Smokey. They were down from Sac and supposed to take Joe up north for a court appearance. They went up to the house after it happened."

"What do you know about John Watson?" Drew asked.

"Oh, yeah, Johnny. Johnny got pissed at Joe because he gave him such a meager split from the Dunn robbery. He only gave me a small amount too, but I didn't complain like Johnny. Man, Joe fucking killed people. He was way out of my league."

"You still haven't told us who you think did the murders," Drew said, squeezing Farmer for anything else he knew.

"Dude, I have to say it was probably Dunn getting even for the robbery. I mean, Joe scared everybody, but he didn't scare Dunn, and I think Dunn did it out of revenge and he wanted his stuff back."

Drew and Estrada felt content with what Farmer had told them. He had given them little new information, but had confirmed some things Dennis Mack had told them. And they could find Farmer easily enough if they wanted to come back to him.

Drew signaled the jailer that they had finished and he came into the room to take Farmer back to lockup.

"We'll probably be back to talk to you more," Drew said to Farmer. He noted Farmer seemed disappointed to hear it.

Chapter Thirteen

THE DETECTIVES SPENT the next three days trying to track down John Watson, but without success. He was in the wind. Next to Dunn, Watson was the guy Drew most wanted to talk to. According to Dennis Mack, Watson had helped facilitate the Dunn robbery for the Wonderland gang, and Mack thought Watson had then rolled over on them and probably had let Dunn's crew into the Wonderland house with the key Harlan Tate's girlfriend, Nancy Poole, had given Watson.

Back at the office, Drew's phone rang. When he picked it up, he found the caller was Lou Moreno, his boss.

"We picked up John Watson at a motel in the San Fernando Valley," Moreno said.

"Where is he now?" Drew said, eager to interview the guy they had been searching for.

"Two other Homicide Special detectives are talking to him. I think he is about to give up the killers. I have to go, Drew. But I'm on the way back to the office. I'll fill you in on the details when I get there." Moreno disconnected the call.

Drew was incredulous and slammed down the phone.

"What's up, Howie?" Li asked, picking up on Drew's sudden anger. Estrada had also noticed and had got up from and his desk and walked over.

"That was Moreno on the phone. He just told me they found John Watson in a motel in the San Fernando Valley and two other Homicide Special detectives are interviewing him."

Li and Estrada stared at Drew in disbelief. "What the fuck?" Li said.

"Exactly," Drew said. "Moreno is on his way back here and I'm going to get some answers."

Moreno walked into the squad room fifteen minutes after the phone call. Drew, Li, and Estrada intercepted him before he got to his office.

"Who is talking to Watson and where is he?" Drew demanded. "He's part of our case. He's a central actor in our case."

Moreno held up his hands in mock surrender. "It's your case, but this has to be a team effort, Drew. Calm down. The guys interviewing Watson might get a confession or at least more information on the killers."

"We should interview Watson," Drew insisted. "We have all the facts and the best grasp of the evidence. Now where is he?"

Under most circumstances, Drew and his team were happy to take all the help they could get. But they needed to take the lead on Watson. Having other detectives stepping in was a serious departure from protocol, not to mention a slap in the face to Drew and his team, the primary investigators. After more prodding and hard words from Drew that bordered on insubordination, Moreno finally revealed that the other Homicide Special detectives had Watson at the Bonaventure Hotel with his girlfriend, Bianca, and his wife, Angela.

"Metro Division is guarding him," Moreno added.

"What the fuck, Lieutenant?" Estrada exclaimed. "Are you taking us off the case?"

Estrada's forceful remark caught Drew off guard. He still assumed Estrada was Moreno's eyes and ears on the team to keep a tight rein on Drew and Li. But Estrada was clearly as upset as he was about the developments and dismayed Moreno was tolerating such a transgression on their investigation.

"No, I already told you, it's your case. But Curtis Cobb and Andy Neal are veteran Homicide Special detectives and skilled interrogators. They found Watson and I think are best positioned to get him to talk."

"We're going down there," Drew said stubbornly, then he and his team headed for the door.

Moreno called after them. "Drew, you aren't getting into the room with Watson. I told you, Cobb and Neal are doing the interview." His parting shot only angered the three detectives further.

On the way to the Bonaventure Hotel, Estrada told Drew he was thinking about dropping out of the case because it was turning into a muddled and mismanaged mess. After they arrived at the hotel, the team's stay was brief. The Metro Division tactical officers didn't approve of the site, complaining there were too many points of ingress and egress for them to secure adequately, and too many people involved. Incredibly, John Watson was also complaining his room was too small.

Drew knew they were expected to cooperate with whatever their bosses came up with, no matter how poor their judgement. To that end, he told the commander of the Metro Division squad he knew a retired LAPD supervisor who worked as a security consultant at the Biltmore Hotel a few blocks away and could get them a more easily secured site there. The Metro detail approved and Drew called his contact, who offered him the use of the vice-presidential suite.

A half hour later, they completed the move. Watson and his two companions made themselves at home in the new opulent surroundings. The two women had seemingly formed an alliance. Getting the new site got Drew and his team into the room, but Cobb and Neal were still going to interview Watson.

While Drew and his team still seethed over the interference with their case, Watson picked up the phone to order room service. He favored expensive single-malt scotch and expected to get it compliments of the LAPD. The idea behind the room was to make Watson comfortable and at ease so he would loosen up and talk. But he had pushed things a bridge too far by ordering the expensive liquor and Drew promptly called and cut off the scotch.

Drew respected Detective Curtis Cobb and his seniority in Homicide Special, and Lou Moreno believed Cobb's cool and level-headed demeanor would gain Watson's confidence and prompt him to open up. But regardless of that, the situation did not sit well with Drew or his team. Cobb was unquestionably an outstanding homicide investigator with a great deal of experience, but the responsibility for the case rested on the collective shoulders of Drew, Li, and Estrada and they felt they were losing control of it.

Cobb spent a considerable amount of time schmoozing Watson, and Watson seemed to grow more and more at ease. Eventually, he told Cobb he would discuss details about the killers and the motive for the murders, but only if the detectives made sure he and the two women got put into a witness protection program. Cobb readily agreed, knowing he had no control over such a decision. Covering himself, he merely promised Watson he would do anything and everything in his power to make it happen.

Watson began his story by admitting to his complicity in the Dunn robbery.

"I drew a diagram of the Dunn residence for Joe Allen and his crew," Watson said. "And I left a sliding glass patio door unlocked for them to get into the house."

"Did you receive a cut after the robbery?" Cobb asked.

"Yeah, Joe gave me two thousand in cash and some coke from Dunn's safe."

"What was your relationship with Tony Dunn? You spend a lot of time at his house?"

Watson nodded. "We got along. I scored coke there often, and I fenced stolen property there from time to time."

"Did Dunn know it was the Wonderland crew that hit his house?" Cobb asked.

"Not when it went down," Watson said. "He knew Joe Allen and Harlan Tate. They had done business. But they went in wearing ski masks to conceal their identities. Dennis Mack, a biker guy Joe brought down from Sacramento to help with the business, did all the talking and Dunn didn't know him."

"But Dunn tumbled to it later?"

"Yeah, some dude he knew heard it was Joe and his crew and told him. Then he became suspicious that I had been in on it because I never made it a secret that I hung out with the crew up at Wonderland."

"So Dunn was behind the hit at Wonderland?"

Watson nodded. "They had humiliated Dunn by robbing his house and making him beg for his life. He wanted revenge, and he wanted the drugs and money back they stole from him."

"You said he became suspicious of you. Did he threaten you or anything?"

"Hell, yes. I dropped by his house to score some coke the next day and he slapped me around. I thought Tony was going to kill me. To get out of it, he made me agree to go to Wonderland and to leave the front door unlocked the morning of the murders."

"So, you were there when it went down?"

"No, I only unlocked the front door using a key Harlan's girlfriend, Nancy, had given me. Then I split. Believe me, man. Tony forced me to do it. He said he would kill me if I didn't cooperate. And I didn't know they were going to kill everyone. I thought Dunn's people would only rough them up and take back Dunn's stuff. Make a statement, you know?"

"Okay, tell me about Dunn's crew, the people who did the killing at Wonderland."

Watson shook his head. "I'm not naming names or giving you the details until we're safe in a witness protection program. If they find out I rolled over on them, they will kill us just like they did Joe's crew."

"Look, John," Cobb said. "I'm going to be straight with you. You need to cooperate with us. Otherwise, even if all you did was unlock the door for the killers to give them access to the house, a murder prosecution could be in your future. You were part of the conspiracy."

"I told you I had no choice. Dunn coerced me. He threatened to kill me."

Cobb shook his head. "Duress is not a defense to conspiracy to commit murder and I have to believe you knew the intentions of the people who entered the Wonderland house. You just alluded to thinking they intended to do bodily injury, even if you didn't know they intended to murder everyone in the house."

"I'm not telling you shit until we're in a witness protection program," Watson insisted stubbornly. "These people will kill us if they find out I burned them."

Drew sighed and eyed his partners. Then he jerked his head towards the front door of the suite. Li and Estrada followed him out.

"Watson won't tell them anything useful," Drew said. "We're just wasting our time here. Let's get back to work."

Cobb and Neal kept Watson at the Biltmore talking for the next five days, five full days of nonsense with Watson and the women. Watson played his role to the hilt, ordering room service several times a day on the LAPD tab and demanding special treatment. Meanwhile, Drew and Estrada complained to Lou Moreno daily about the interference with their case. They didn't believe

Cobb's VIP kid-gloves strategy with John Watson would yield any useful information that would help them solve the case. Drew believed getting Watson out of the Biltmore and treating him like any other witness instead of like a celebrity would be more effective.

Eventually, claustrophobia set in for the occupants of the Biltmore suite and friction developed between Watson's girlfriend and wife, for obvious reasons. Angela Watson was the first to leave. She packed up her belongings and headed home to Glendale.

The morning of the sixth day, with no progress occurring, Moreno, with the approval of his boss, released Watson to deal with the felony theft charge they had picked him up on and he got out of custody on his own recognizance without posting bail. Watson got his wife's car out of the impound lot and was in the wind again. But not for long.

Chapter Fourteen

THE DAY MORENO KICKED Watson, Drew and his team adopted a new strategy. Every evening after leaving the PAB, one of them spent several hours at staggered times each evening parked or driving near Tony Dunn's house, checking for activity and monitoring those coming and going from the residence. Captain Meyers might have forbidden them from talking to Dunn, but he couldn't prevent the detectives from monitoring and documenting the activity at the man's house.

Things like recording license plate numbers of the vehicles at the home and checking them later for owner information and knowing what was going on at the location on particular dates and times provided bits of intelligence that could help them fill in many blanks later on.

On the very day John Watson got kicked loose from the Biltmore, while Drew was staking out the residence, Watson showed up at Dunn's house. After he had told Cobb the details of his participation in the Dunn robbery and the murders, Drew wondered if Watson shared any of those supposedly factual details with Dunn. He presumed the man had not. Drew assumed the chances of that happening were as small as the chances of Watson ever voluntarily testifying in court.

Another evening, while Li was taking her turn surveilling the Dunn home, she had jotted down a license plate number. After checking the registration the following morning, she learned the car belonged to a well-known local newspaper reporter who had been covering the Wonderland murders.

Two weeks after the murders, Drew received another unexpected relevant contact, this time an email from a retired Hollywood Station patrol officer. The former officer wrote that while working patrol in the division in 2016, he had responded to many criminal complaints at the Fiction nightclub on

Sunset Boulevard, a club owned by Tony Dunn. His email described how many people had wanted to make assault complaints against the club's main bouncer, Justin Carr, but got talked out of following through with formal complaints. The email said the complainants had stated Carr had assaulted them with a nightstick or similar type of impact weapon.

The retired officer said he had never recovered a weapon during the calls. But he wrote that he later made a traffic stop on Dunn's vehicle the evening of one reported assault pursuant to the complaints he had received. He stated that during a search of Dunn's vehicle that he found a length of steel pipe with one end encased by a rubber bicycle handlebar grip. The former officer stated he had arrested Dunn and booked him on a possession of a deadly weapon charge and later Dunn got convicted in municipal court on the charge.

The information the retired LAPD officer provided showed at least a circumstantial evidentiary link between Dunn and the purported type of weapons used in the Wonderland killings. Drew filed it for future use.

Drew had a surprise waiting for him when he picked up his phone from the kitchen breakfast bar to take a call. It was a Sunday morning in November, four months into the investigation. Progress had slowed to a crawl, and Drew and his team were now taking weekend days off.

"Howard Drew," the male caller said after Drew answered. "I don't know if you remember me, but this is Ryan Norman, North Hollywood Division."

The name sounded familiar, but no face came to mind for Drew. But he wouldn't be obvious about not remembering the North Hollywood detective.

"Yeah, Ryan. What's up?"

"We're out on a DB call at 3418 Mountcastle Drive in Studio City. You interested?"

By now, the address of Tony Dunn was not only familiar to Drew, but to most LAPD cops and anyone else who read a newspaper because of the ongoing Wonderland investigation. The North Hollywood detective had assumed RHD would want to respond and handle the investigation.

"Yeah, I'm interested. Who's the stiff?"

"We haven't identified the body yet. Black male, but it isn't Dunn. We didn't want to touch anything that might connect to the Wonderland murders without checking first."

"Good call. I'll call my partners. Give us twenty minutes."

"You got it, Howard."

Drew disconnected and called Li and Estrada, both of whom agreed to meet him at Dunn's home. He pulled on his hiking boots, shrugged into his LAPD windbreaker, grabbed his badge and service weapon, and headed out the door. Finally, he had his chance to talk to Dunn, Captain Meyers be damned.

Chapter Fifteen

FIFTEEN MINUTES LATER, Drew pulled to the curb in front of Dunn's home. Li and Estrada hadn't arrived yet. Understandable since Drew lived less than five miles away. It had taken longer to phone his partners and get dressed than it had to drive over. Two North Hollywood detectives met him on the driveway inside the open sliding gate. Drew recognized Norman. He guessed he had met him before. Norman introduced his partner, Neal Lowe.

"We didn't start anything," Norman explained. "The DB is in the guest bedroom on the bed. Looks like an OD. The paramedics already pronounced him and we told them we would let the coroner's office handle the transport. Soon as we realized whose house it was, we backed off, and I called you."

Li stopped out in front of the house, and Estrada pulled in right behind her. They got out and joined Drew and the North Hollywood detectives on the driveway. Drew made the introductions and then told Norman they would take over.

"He's expecting you," Norman said. "We told him the downtown detectives were going to do the investigation."

Drew nodded. "Thanks again."

Drew, Li, and Estrada headed to the front door and the two North Hollywood detectives to their car.

As they entered the foyer, the detectives looked around and noticed things looked different. Of course, no flash-bang grenades had just detonated inside the living room this time, but the house looked more than just clean. It looked suspiciously immaculate. Nothing was lying on the floor, everything was in its proper place, and they even heard the dishwasher running. All appeared in order, except for the dead body the detectives had come to investigate.

Dunn appeared agitated when he recognized the three detectives, remembering they had been to his house during the warrant service raid months before. Now they were back to investigate a death in his house. He led them down the hallway to the guest bedroom, remaining in the hallway when they walked into the bedroom. The body of a black male who looked like he had been mid to late twenties lay supine on the bed. Li picked up a wallet from the nightstand beside the bed and checked it for identification. Estrada, standing beside the bed, leaned over and examined the victim.

"Who was he?" Drew asked Dunn.

"Demond Fabrizia."

"Friend of yours?"

"An employee. He was a sound technician at Fiction, my club on Sunset Boulevard."

"What was he doing here?"

"He was visiting."

"Was he in here alone?"

"Aayla was in the room with him."

"The zombie in the living room?"

Dunn's jaw clenched. "That's Aayla Campbell in the living room. She lives here. Aayla found him like this when she woke up. She woke me and I called nine-one-one, but it was too late."

"It's an OD, Howie," Estrada said.

"Demond Fabrizia, age twenty-six," Li said, holding a California driver's license she had found in the wallet. "There's a fit kit on the nightstand. Probably heroin."

"Demond had a heroin problem," Dunn said calmly, as if speaking of a normal medical condition.

Drew walked over and inspected the body. He lifted an arm a few inches by the wrist. Fabrizia had been bleeding profusely from the nose before he died and the body was in full rigor. That told Drew he had probably been dead for well over twelve hours. The room looked like someone had cleaned it thoroughly. It looked a little too pristine for a room where two heroin addicts had spent the night. Drew wasn't buying it that the dead guy was shooting up while the woman just slept through the whole thing. The scene looked staged.

Drew asked Dunn to return to the living room, then the three detectives huddled up.

"It could have been a hot shot administered by persons unknown intending to kill him," Estrada said.

"If he did something to piss off Dunn, this would probably be the way Dunn would have taken him out," Li said. "And someone staged the scene."

"I don't disagree," Drew said. "It could have been a deliberate overdose. But it's possible they cleaned up to keep Dunn out of another narcotics beef."

"We could lock the place down and get a search warrant," Estrada suggested.

"I could broaden the scope of the affidavit to include Fabrizia's workplace just to squeeze Dunn a little harder," Li said.

Drew thought it over. But seeing as how Dunn and his crew had gone over the premises before they had arrived, he figured getting a warrant and doing a search would probably be a waste of time. And he didn't want it to appear they were harassing Dunn just for the sake of it. Drew wanted to nail Dunn for the Wonderland murders, but he wanted the evidence in the case to do the talking and not some harassment-driven accusation.

After talking it over and looking at all the angles, the detectives decided to write it up as an undetermined cause of death, pending the autopsy. They knew it was very hard to prove a hot shot case without direct witness testimony or physical evidence to corroborate their suspicions. They would let the coroner's office make the call.

Regardless, Drew's gut told him Fabrizia had received a hot shot for upsetting the wrong guy, and the wrong guy was Dunn. But the hard evidence just wasn't there and he couldn't prove it.

Chapter Sixteen

THE WONDERLAND CASE was stymied, and Drew grew more frustrated by the day. They needed to catch a break of some kind to recapture momentum. Back at their desks, Li was finishing up a report on a telephone interview and Drew was working the phones. Estrada was out of the office in court on another homicide case he had worked before joining the team.

Clearly, two central figures had emerged as persons of interest in the investigation, Tony Dunn and John Watson. Dunn remained off limits for Drew to interview, but there was a recent development with Watson. A latent print identification.

Specialists at the Scientific Investigation Division's Latent Print Unit, historically always backlogged, were still analyzing and running the latent prints lifted at the crime scene through automated databases. And they had identified recently a partial, bloody left-hand palm print lifted from the ornate bed railing above the battered body of Joe Allen as belonging to John Watson.

The report from the unit Drew had received noted a criminalist at the scene had lifted the print from a position consistent with someone using the bed railing to brace himself as he struck down on the head of Joe Allen. The print identification, along with the fact the print put John Watson in the crime scene at the time of the murders, provided a basis for Drew to bring Watson in for questioning again. This time, a proper interrogation after Detective Curtis Cobb's abysmal failure when he interviewed Watson in the luxurious confines of the Biltmore Hotel suite. But while the team knew Dunn's whereabouts all the time, Watson's had proven tougher to nail down. The detectives were still surveilling Dunn's Studio City home, and no one had seen Watson visiting the house in months.

Drew had confirmed a department rumor that Watson was a high-end confidential informant for the Vice Division, the LAPD unit responsible for investigating, among other things, pornography crimes. He had learned from a vice cop he knew that Detective Ray Tucker at the Vice Division handled

Watson. Drew wanted to talk with Tucker to see if he would help the RHD detectives run down Watson's current whereabouts. He was aware it was a long shot because he knew vice officers rarely gave up their sources to anyone.

"You ready for lunch, Howie?" Li asked, shutting down her computer.

"Sure, but I want to stop by Fort Davis first to speak to a vice detective about John Watson." Fort Davis, named for former chief Ed Davis, on East Fifth Street was the home of the Central Division of the LAPD and the home of the Vice Division.

"Watson's handler?" Li asked. Drew had already told her about discovering Watson's status as a confidential informant.

"Yeah, Ray Tucker."

"You know vice cops don't give up their sources, Howie. It's a waste of time."

"I only want to ask him to help us locate Watson," Drew countered. "It has nothing to do with his status as a CI."

Li shrugged. "Whatever, Howie. Since we'll be in the neighborhood anyway, we can have lunch at Cole's afterward."

"You're on, Amy," Drew said, putting on his jacket. And the detectives left the office.

When they arrived at Fort Davis, Li parked their ride and they went inside. While Drew didn't know Ray Tucker personally, he knew Tucker was a senior investigator in the Vice Division and had a solid reputation, although Drew had heard the man could be brusque occasionally. After they asked at the front desk to see Tucker, he walked out to meet them in the lobby, where they exchanged introductions. Tucker then escorted them back to his office.

Case files, photographs, and a lot more cluttered the office and Tucker's appearance screamed lax grooming and dress standards, but Drew knew the man was a respected veteran detective who had been around the block more than a few times. While Tucker's dress wasn't out of GQ, he seemed affable enough. Once they had all sat down, Drew got right to the point and asked about Watson in a general way. Drew had no intention of throwing his RHD weight around as he sensed from Tucker's demeanor that he was a savvy street cop and no pushover. Drew figured if he wanted a favor from Tucker, it would be smart to show some respect for him and his position.

"I know John pretty well," Tucker acknowledged in reply to Drew's question.

"Watson is a person of interest in the murder case we're working," Drew explained. "We would appreciate getting everything you have on him. Associates, vehicles, where he scores, association with Tony Dunn, and any other criminal figures. And of course, where he is now."

Tucker leaned back in his chair with his feet on top of his desk, held up his open hands in a gesture of helplessness. "Try to see it from my position, Detectives," he said. "Watson has been a solid informant, and he's given us a lot of solid intelligence. My lieutenant and captain both like the information I've got using Watson. That information has made everyone happy all the way up to the chief."

"We're asking you to see it from our position," Drew countered. "Like I said, we're working a vicious quadruple murder that could soon have a fifth dead victim. We have a bloody latent print lifted from the scene showing Watson was there during the murders."

"The media are all over the case," Li added. "I'm sure they would love hearing Watson was a snitch for the LAPD and that Vice Division is protecting him because he helped you make porn cases."

"You think the chief would be happy to go along with covering for Watson if a media story like that hit the papers and television?" Drew asked.

Drew was sure he saw a light come on in Tucker's eyes, the tough, street-wise vice cop. He removed his feet from the top of his desk and sat up.

"Okay, Detectives, I get it," he said. "I'll run Watson down for you, but sometimes he's hard to find. He moves around a lot. But I understand. No one wants to see anyone embarrassed, including the chief, over a porn snitch."

Any good detective would try to protect their informant at almost any cost. But clearly, the Wonderland case was a unique situation, and Tucker had been around long enough to know it was time to blink.

Chapter Seventeen

TWO WEEKS LATER, BACK in the RHD squad room, Drew and his team were reviewing what they had so far and where they should go next with the investigation. The question of Watson's whereabouts still lingered. They had had heard nothing from Ray Tucker over at Vice Division and Drew had concluded no help was coming from that quarter.

"He has grand theft and receiving stolen property charges pending," Estrada pointed out. "Why don't we put out an NCIC want on Watson? Maybe we'll get lucky and get him picked up on a traffic stop."

"Good idea," Drew agreed. "We should also put the wanted notice out to the fugitive detail, the airport detail, LASD, and all LAPD divisions."

"Angela Watson, his wife is still on the interview list," Li offered. "I updated the list yesterday, and she still lives in Glendale. Maybe she has heard from Watson."

"Good point, Amy," Drew said. "Tell you what, Oscar, why don't you put together the wanted notice and roll with it? Amy and I will drive up to Glendale to talk to Watson's wife. She might feel more comfortable having a female officer on the visit."

Estrada agreed and Drew and Li left for Glendale to visit with John Watson's wife, Angela. The detectives assumed John Watson was on the run with his girlfriend Bianca Schumer, but believed it possible he might have contacted Angela.

Thirty minutes after leaving downtown LA, Drew pulled to the curb in front of the Watson home, a modest white frame and stucco on Linden Avenue in Glendale. The detectives took the stair-stepped tiled walk to the porch and knocked on the door. They recognized Angela Watson when she opened it.

"Ms. Watson," Li said. "I'm LAPD Detective Li and this is my partner, Detective Drew. Do you have a few moments you could spare to talk with us?"

To their surprise, Angela Watson was both polite and cordial. She invited them in.

"I remember seeing you both at the Biltmore Hotel," Angela said after they were all seated in the living room. "I suppose you're here to talk about John."

"Yes, that's correct," Li said. "There has been a development in the case, and we want to talk to your husband about it. Do you know where John is?"

"I don't," Angela said. "I suppose you expect me to say that whether or not I do. But I really don't know. About all I can tell you is he is driving my car." She provided the car's make and model and the license plate number. The woman appeared sincere to the detectives and seemed cooperative.

"Any idea where he might stay if he's still in the Los Angeles area?" Drew asked.

"John has friends all over Southern California and has family living in Ohio. As far as local, he has a very close relationship with Bill Willis, a porn director John has worked for quite a bit. He lives out in the San Fernando Valley. I always found Bill boorish and didn't care for him personally. But he and John are close, and I'm sure Bill would let him stay at his place."

Referring to the time of the murders and before the debacle at the Biltmore, Drew asked Angela Watson when she last saw her husband around that time.

"It was on July second," she replied.

"What were the circumstances?" Drew prodded.

"Well, he came here to the house. He was bloody and bruised and asked me to draw a bath for him. John told me he had been at the Wonderland house, the house where those people got murdered."

"What was his mental state at the time?" Li asked. "How did he act?"

"John seemed scared, and I had never seen him so upset. He didn't tell me any details. John just said that was where he had come from and I didn't ask questions. I didn't want to upset him more than he already was. John can be a little unpredictable when he gets stressed about something."

Angela Watson appeared forthright, and both detectives believed she had only confused the second of July with the first. But they didn't press her on it. Whether or not she had confused the dates, they both knew it was irrelevant.

They both knew Angela Watson would never testify to anything regarding John Watson in a court of law. And the law could not compel her to do so.

"Have you heard from John recently?" Li asked.

"John called me several weeks ago," Angela admitted. "He told me he was in Pendleton, Oregon. He said he needed money, but I told him I didn't have any money to send him."

"Why would he go to Oregon?" Drew asked.

"Bianca, his girlfriend, has family there. Since he said he needed cash, I assumed they went up there because they ran out of money."

Satisfied that Angela Watson had told them all she knew, or at least would share, the detectives thanked her for her time and left. Drew had given her a business card and asked her to call if she heard from her husband, but he wasn't confident she would.

They got back in the car for the drive back to LA.

"You think she was just confused about the date of the day he came home bloody from Wonderland?" Li asked.

"I'm willing to give her the benefit of the doubt," Drew said. "She didn't appear she was being deceptive about anything she told us. But I got the feeling she probably knew more than she was willing to tell."

"Doesn't matter," Li said. "Spouses don't have to testify against each other."

"True."

"You think he could still be in Oregon?"

"Don't know," Drew said. "But it's the only lead we have. It's probably worth checking out."

"Are we all going?" Li asked.

"No, two of us will go."

"You taking me or Oscar?"

"You."

Li grinned. "Because you know I'm the better detective, right?"

Drew smiled back. "Because if I take you, policy allows us to get separate rooms. If I took Oscar, we would have to room together."

"Well, at least you were honest about it," Li said, laughing.

Chapter Eighteen

IN ANY HIGH-PROFILE case, many tips came in all the time. Since the three detectives couldn't possibly follow them all to a conclusion, they only followed those that seemed most promising. Such was the case with the tip from Angela Watson. It was the only lead they had on John Watson's whereabouts. And even if he was no longer in Pendleton, Oregon, perhaps his girlfriend's relatives would tell them where the couple had gone.

Two days after interviewing Angela Watson, Drew and Li left LAX on a national carrier for Portland, Oregon. There, they would connect with a small regional airline for the last leg of their trip to Pendleton.

It was a frigid day when they arrived in the small Oregon town with a population of about seventeen thousand. Having never heard of the town, Drew had looked it up on the internet and learned that the population included the sixteen hundred inmates at the Eastern Oregon Correctional Institution located in Pendleton.

While Drew and Li were in the air bound for Oregon, Oscar Estrada headed to Cedars-Sinai Hospital. Drew had transferred responsibility for Dawn Allen, their only potential witness to the murders, from Li to Estrada. That was because after coordinating the pathologist's examination of Allen with her attending physician, neurologist Dr. Marc Cohen, Estrada had earned the trust of Dr. Cohen, who was ever protective of his patient. Drew decided Estrada would continue as Dawn Allen's lone contact with the LAPD. Dr. Cohen had called Estrada and told him Dawn was awake and able to communicate on a limited basis. So, Estrada left for the hospital immediately, eager to learn if he could glean any information from the sole survivor of the bloody massacre at Wonderland.

After renting a car, Li and Drew drove to the Pendleton Police Department on Airport Road. They met with a detective there who tracked down the address of Bianca Schumer's parents for them. It was a small town, but there were many people with the last name Schumer living there. With the address in hand, they drove out to the address on the east edge of town that the detective had given them.

Bianca Schumer's family was welcoming and cooperative, but the detectives hadn't been in town two hours before learning Angela Watson's information about John was stale. The parents had seemed forthright and eager for the police to take John into custody so that their daughter would be safe. They gave Drew and Li the address of their son, Frank, Bianca's younger brother, and the detectives drove there to speak with him.

Frank Schumer told the LA detectives that he and his sister were close and that he was very upset with Watson because John had beaten his sister several times. He said his sister lied about it, but he had seen the bruises that revealed the truth. Frank also told them Watson and his sister had arrived in her car and Watson had repainted it a new color, probably as an attempt to disguise it and evade capture. The detectives assumed Watson must have sold his wife's car to get traveling money.

Drew and Li also learned from Frank Schumer that Watson and Bianca had been in Pendleton only briefly before taking off. Frank said he had overheard them talking about going to Montana, but didn't know where they had planned to go in the state.

While Watson was still in the wind and already long gone when they arrived in Oregon, Drew didn't consider the trip a complete waste of time. The detectives had formed a positive relationship with Frank Schumer, who told them he expected he would hear from his sister and would contact them when he learned where she and Watson were.

Since the media was heavily involved with the case, back in Los Angeles, Drew and his team were still receiving dozens of tips on Watson that had to be checked out. Like all experienced investigators who had handled hundreds and sometimes thousands of such tips while working high-profile cases, the team adopted a system to deal with the never-ending flow. They assigned priority numbers one through three to each tip as they came in. One meant they would give immediate attention to the tip because it appeared to be a solid lead. A two was a tip that seemed important enough for them to follow up on, but that seemed less promising than a tip coded as a one. A tip assigned a three was one the detectives considered roughly the equivalent of a UFO sighting report, and they gave those types no attention. It was only a matter of days after Drew and Li had returned from Oregon before the team received a tip they categorized as a solid one.

Amy Li had kept in touch with Bianca Schumer's family in Oregon, especially her brother Frank. She kept reminding Frank that he could be a tremendous asset in helping to get his sister away from Watson and explained she believed Bianca's life was in danger as long as she was with Watson. Frank seemed motivated to help his sister, and by extension, the LAPD detectives, in any way he could.

Less than a week after they had spoken with Frank in Oregon, he called Li and told her he had received a collect call from his sister from somewhere in the area of North Miami Beach in northern Dade County, Florida. Schumer gave Li the telephone number from his phone bill and she traced it to a phone registered to a real estate office in Surfside, Florida.

To Li's surprise, Frank Schumer offered to meet the detectives in Miami, telling her he had lived in the Miami area for several years and had attended high school there. He still had acquaintances there and knew the area well.

Once Li discussed the developments with Drew, he agreed they needed to fly to Miami and signed off on the plan to use Frank Schumer's help to locate his sister Bianca, an effort that the detectives hoped would end with the apprehension of John Watson.

Once again, Drew and Li would make the out-of-state trip, this time to Florida while Estrada stayed in Los Angeles. Dawn Allen continued to show signs of improvement, and Dr. Cohen had told Estrada he believed Dawn was strong enough for him to interview her again. The first attempt Estrada had made to interview her while Drew and LI were in Oregon had disappointed. Allen had been too confused to tell him anything and had instead only asked questions about what had happened to her and when she could go home. This time, Estrada hoped he could begin winning her trust and learn something useful. The team had agreed having one dedicated member of the investigation as her confidant would work best for Allen because of her still delicate medical condition.

Chapter Nineteen

DREW AND LI TOOK A noon flight to Miami International on the last day of November, planning to meet Frank Schumer when they arrived. After calling Frank's cell phone, they met him in the terminal and then rented a car. After dropping Schumer off at the home of a couple in a suburban area northwest of Miami who had befriended the Schumers years before and whose children had attended school with Frank and Bianca, Drew and Li checked into their hotel.

It was part of the RHD's travel protocol for detectives to check in with the locals and explain what they were in town for and where they planned to go. Partly, it was just a simple courtesy, but the LAPD detectives had no jurisdiction in Florida and would need the help of local enforcement to take Watson into custody if they found him. So early in the morning on the first of December, exactly five months after the Wonderland murders, Drew pulled their rental car to the curb in front of the Surfside Police Department on Harding Avenue. They would begin the search in Surfside because the collect telephone call from Bianca Schumer to her brother originated from the town.

The Surfside Police Department had thirty-one sworn officers, one of whom was Detective Liz Tracy, one of the five detectives on the force. She had nine years of service with the department. And when Drew asked the uniformed officer at the front desk to speak to with someone from the detective bureau, Tracy was the detective who came to the lobby to greet them. They shook hands all around after Drew and Li showed her their badges and identification and told her why they were in town.

"Did you guys call ahead?" Tracy asked. "The captain mentioned nothing to us about it."

"No, we just showed up," Drew said. "We got a tip the guy we're looking for was in the area and jumped on a plane yesterday and flew down here."

Tracy nodded. She looked like a capable and experienced law enforcement officer. She was early thirties and fit, with long brown hair pulled into a ponytail and wore a gray women's business suit.

"Who are we talking about here?" she asked.

"A suspect in a quadruple murder case we're working," Drew said. "We understand he is in the area with his girlfriend from LA and we want to take him into custody if we can locate him."

"I see," Tracy said. "This guy have a name?"

"John Curtis Watson," Li said. "He's a thirty-nine-year-old white male, six feet two, thin build, with brown curly hair."

"John Watson," Tracy mused. "Why does that name sound familiar?"

"He is something of a celebrity in the pornography industry back in LA," Li smirked.

Tracy's eyes opened wide, her eyebrows raised, and her jaw dropped. "That John Watson?" Then she winked at Li. "Sounds like you guys get a lot more interesting cases in Los Angeles than the steady diet of property crimes and muggings I'm usually working."

"We have little to go on right now," Drew said. "There's a realty office here in town we want to check out. Beyond that, we're planning on trying to locate the girlfriend, Bianca Schumer, hoping she will lead us to Watson." Drew gave her the name of the realty office where Bianca had used a telephone.

"Oh, sure, I know of it. It's on Collins Avenue, less than five minutes from the station. I'll take you out there if you want. I just need to run back up to the squad room first and let my supervisor know."

Tracy drove. The realty office that Bianca Schumer's call originated from was a four-minute drive away, south on Harding Avenue and then a left to jog north a block on Collins Avenue, a parallel street. Drew was in the backseat, having given Li the front. Tracy pulled into a strip mall and parked in front of the realty office. The detectives got out and went inside.

The detectives interviewed the three employees in the office separately. None could identity Watson or Schumer from the photos the LAPD detectives had with them on their phones, and all claimed they didn't know anyone named John Watson or Bianca Schumer. All three also claimed to know nothing about the phone call made from their business. They all mentioned having a telephone readily available for use by visitors to the office, but claimed they didn't allow people who just walked in off the street to use it. Since the phone in question wasn't under constant observation, it appeared that was exactly what had happened.

After the dry hole, Tracy drove them back to the police station to regroup. They discussed the possibility of showing Watson and Schumer's photos around the hotels in the area, but shelved the idea as impractical. Drew told Tracy they would nose around a little on their own and contact her if they found something and needed help from the local cops. Tracy told them that her ex-husband, David Tracy, was a detective with the Metro-Dade Police just north of Surfside. She believed he would help Drew and Li in his jurisdiction if they needed it. The detectives exchanged cell phone numbers and the LA murder cops left the station.

Back in the rental car, Li called Frank Schumer while Drew drove. He told her he had some information on his sister and Li told him they would pick him up. Frank was waiting on the front porch of the house where they had dropped him off the previous evening when they arrived. He walked out and got into the backseat of the rental.

"I told them I was in town looking for Bianca and asked if they had seen her. They said they had. Bianca dropped by their house with another young woman about two weeks ago."

"Did she tell them where she lived or worked?" Drew asked.

"Not exactly. Bianca told them her friend worked as a dancer at a club called the Foxy Lady in Coral Gables. And she said she was living with her friend temporarily and helping care for her children. After the visit, they said Bianca and the other woman drove off in an usual-looking Ford pickup truck. They said it looked like an amateur had repainted the truck blue."

"Did they know the friend's name?"

"Just her first name, Aubrey. But they gave me a pretty good description."

It appeared to Drew and Li that they had their first solid lead in locating Bianca Schumer.

Drew and Li dropped Frank off at the Palms Beach Motel, on the way to the Metro-Dade's Northeast Station. They told him they would call him as soon as they found out where Bianca was living. They were concerned about not putting Frank in jeopardy, but since he and his sister were close, they believed she might listen to her brother and cooperate with them when they found her. After dropping Frank, they continued to the Metro-Dade station to talk with Detective David Tracy.

Chapter Twenty

DREW AND LI ENTERED the lobby of the Northeast Station and asked for Detective Tracy. A few minutes later, David Tracy came out and introduced himself. He was in his mid-thirties with boyish looks and a reserved manner, which Drew found unusual for a detective. Tracy looked like anything but a cop, and Drew figured he would be perfect for undercover work.

Tracy took them upstairs to his workstation and got down to work. He found that the Foxy Lady had dancers working every night, and the club was open until three each morning. Drew and Li planned to go there that night to locate Bianca Schumer's friend Aubrey. If they could locate the blue truck with the unusual paint job, they would stake it out and follow the driver home. Tracy told them if they found the truck and wanted to go inside the club to identify the woman, he would stay outside and watch the truck for them until the club closed. Drew and Li agreed to the plan, and the detectives exchanged cell phone numbers. Drew told Tracy that he and Li would go to the club around midnight and Tracy agreed to meet them there. Then Drew and Li left the station and drove back to their hotel to rest and have dinner before leaving for the club.

After meeting David Tracy in the parking lot of the Foxy Lady, the detectives found the blue Ford pickup truck easily. The paint job was as bad as described. It looked like someone had repainted it with spray paint cans bought from a home improvement store. Tracy positioned his unmarked car where he could keep his eyes on the truck, and Drew and Li entered the club separately. A few minutes after Li entered, Drew sat down beside her at the crowded bar and ordered a draft beer, as Li had done.

The interior of the club boasted three circular stages, accommodating three nude dancers. Club patrons could view the action on the stage platforms from anywhere inside the club. The three dancers were hard at work, gyrating to the earsplitting music blaring from the sound system. Drew and Li didn't have to worry about feigning conversation because of the loud music and other noise. The shouts, whoops, and catcalls from the boisterous, inebriated young male patrons inside the packed club gave the deafening music a run for its money.

The major attraction seemed to be the young woman dancing on the center stage. The curvaceous young woman balanced herself on her hands as she did splits in the air with her legs. She then hand-walked across the platform to the edge and slowly lowered her legs down and around the neck of an elated, intoxicated patron. Drew and Li looked at each other. They had identified Aubrey by the distinctive full-sleeve tattoos that Frank's acquaintances had described. Drew was happy he was a lapsed Catholic, because what the woman did next would have forced him to go to confession just for watching.

A few minutes before one-thirty in the morning, Drew and Li decided to get some fresh air and watch the pickup truck from their rental. The remaining early morning hours dragged on for the cops until the target walked out of the club at ten minutes after three, this time wearing clothes. She walked straight to the truck, accompanied by a young male. They got in the truck and pulled out of the parking lot with the woman driving, headed south on Lejeune Road.

Using cell phones, Li and Tracy stayed in communication. The Metro-Dade detective took the lead on the tail. About five minutes after they left the club, the pickup pulled into the driveway of a darkened home in a Coral Gables neighborhood. The headlights remained on. Tracy continued past and turned right at the next intersection so he could make a U-turn and circle back. Drew had stopped the rental about half a block from the house and extinguished the headlights as soon as he saw the pickup brake and turn into the driveway.

After a few minutes, the pickup truck backed from the driveway and then sped toward Drew and Li's rental at a high rate of speed. Moments later, Tracy's unmarked car blasted past them with the headlights off. Drew made a U-turn to follow, but in seconds, both vehicles disappeared from sight before he made the turn to follow. Tracy told Li over the phone that they were heading north on Lejeune Road. Drew sped north, trying to catch Tracy and the target vehicle. As they passed Majorca Avenue, Drew and Li spotted Tracy's car directly ahead of them, behind the blue truck. They didn't know if the woman had spotted the tail since there was little other traffic on the secondary road at the early morning hour.

After passing the Foxy Lady, the pickup truck with the detectives in tow merged onto a freeway and with more traffic, the tail got easier. Tracy and the two LA cops followed the target vehicle until the woman exited the freeway and pulled into a Denny's restaurant near the Miami International airport and parked. The dancer got out and joined four young males in the parking lot. The five of them then went into the restaurant for what the detectives assumed was an early-morning breakfast.

At four-fifteen, the group exited Denny's, and the woman got back in the pickup truck and headed north on the Miami Turnpike alone. The detectives followed close behind as she exited at NW 182nd Street. The truck turned into a darkened residential area and the detectives backed off and killed their headlights to avoid detection.

The truck finally pulled into the driveway of a single-family house festooned with twinkling Christmas lights. When the dancer killed the truck's lights, got out, and walked into the house, Tracy inched closer to get the address and then continued on past the house. He made a U-turn and circled back to the rental car where Drew had pulled to the curb a few houses down the street.

"Looks like she is home and dry for the night," Tracy said out his open window. He gave Drew the house numbers.

"Yeah, we'll stay and watch the house for a few minutes," Drew said, "but I'm sure you're right. Go get some sleep, Detective, and thanks for your help."

"No problem," Tracy said. "If you find Watson in the Metro-Dade jurisdiction, call me when you're ready to take him down."

"Will do," Drew said. "Thanks again."

Tracy nodded and rolled off into the night.

"Think Bianca Schumer is in the house?" Li asked, as they watched the lights go off inside the house.

"Seems a safe bet she is," Drew said. "We'll follow up in the morning after we get some sleep."

Drew started the car, made a U-turn, and headed for their hotel.

Chapter Twenty-One

A FEW MINUTES BEFORE ten the next morning. Drew and Li left their hotel, heading to the Palms Beach Motel to pick up Frank Schumer, hoping to get him inside his sister's current residence. At ten-thirty, after picking up Frank, they met with Detective David Tracy, who had permission from his supervisor to assist the LAPD detectives. Over a late breakfast at a local restaurant Tracy had recommended, Drew and Li laid out their plan. Frank was to take the detective's rental car and drive to Bianca's friend's home. On arrival, assuming his sister was there, Frank was to do his best to talk Bianca into speaking with the LAPD detectives. Drew and Li would follow Frank with Detective Tracy in his car and park somewhere nearby to wait for his call.

After breakfast, Frank drove the rental car to the address the detectives had given him, with Tracy, Drew, and Li following. Tracy pulled his unmarked car to the curb a half block from the house they had followed the dancer to earlier that morning, close enough so the detectives could see the front of the house. After Frank parked the rental and got out of the car, Tracy pulled out a pair of binoculars and watched Frank approach the front door. He knocked. A few moments later, the front door opened. Even with the binoculars, Tracy couldn't see the person who answered the door. But after only a few moments, Frank entered the house, and the door closed behind him.

"He's in," Tracy said. "His sister is at home."

"Now it's more waiting," Li said. "I hate stakeouts."

Tracy chuckled. Since Tracy was curious to know more about the case they were working, Drew and Li answered some general questions without giving too much away. Homicide detectives didn't share information about an active murder investigation, even with other law enforcement officers not associated with the case. But Tracy had been helpful and Drew didn't want him to think them ungrateful, so he shared some general information with the Metro-Dade detective that anyone in LA could have learned about the Wonderland murders by reading the papers or watching the television news.

Noon came and went without a call from Frank Schumer. Tracy told Drew and Li there was a good burger place about a half mile away, if they wanted to get lunch. Drew felt reluctant to leave Frank alone inside the house, but they all needed a bathroom break. So, Drew agreed but suggested they get takeaway meals and return to the neighborhood to eat in the car.

Tracy drove them to the restaurant, and they all went inside. He placed the food orders while Drew and Li visited the restrooms. Then Drew and Li waited for the food while Tracy took his turn in the restroom. Drew paid for the food and Tracy drove them back to the neighborhood and parked down the street from the house. While they ate, Tracy told the LA cops he worked CAPs, crimes against persons cases, but aspired to become a homicide investigator. The conversation shifted away from the case to a general discussion of LAPD homicide investigation procedures and tactics.

Just before four o'clock in the afternoon, Li's phone rang. She answered and Frank told her that his sister's friend was leaving the house to do some shopping in a few minutes. He said he hadn't sold Bianca completely on the idea, but she had agreed to talk to the detectives while her friend was away from the house.

The detectives watched Aubrey exit the house and get in the Ford pickup truck. She reversed out of the driveway, drove toward them and then past them without a glance toward the unmarked police car. Tracy started the car and then drove toward the house, pulling to the curb one house before they reached it.

"I'll wait out here and will call you if the dancer comes back before you finish," he said.

Drew and Li got out and walked to the front door of the house. Frank was waiting inside the storm door and he opened it and let them in.

"She isn't thrilled with me," Frank whispered before leading the detectives into the living room.

The detectives found Bianca Schumer sitting on a sofa. A male toddler was sitting beside her and she held an infant in her arms she was feeding with a bottle. Drew reintroduced himself and Li.

"I know who you are," Bianca said coldly.

"No one is going to force you to do anything," Li said. "We only ask you to hear us out."

Bianca nodded, but said nothing. But the detectives talked, and she listened. Taking turns, Drew and Li explained the trouble John Watson had got himself into and told Bianca she shouldn't have to shoulder Watson's troubles. They explained she had her entire life ahead of her and the dangers of staying with Watson were real and that she shouldn't let him pull her down with him.

Bianca was defensive at first. "Tony Dunn has threatened John and Dunn has the LA cops in his pocket. Maybe you're working for Dunn. How do I know I can trust you?"

"That's a reasonable question under the circumstances," Drew said. "We've learned during our investigation that there probably are some bent cops on Dunn's payroll. But we don't work for Dunn. We want nothing more than to arrest him for his role in the murders and see him go to prison where he belongs."

Drew saw the young woman's expression had softened a little, but he wasn't sure he had convinced her. But he and Li continued talking with her about John Watson and his untenable position, and she began responding instead of only listening. Li keyed in on Bianca's anger at Watson and his self-centeredness, his ego, and his lies.

"No one wants to hear this, Bianca," Li said kindly. "But John Watson has used you just like he used his wife. You won't have the future you deserve unless you separate yourself from him."

Tears rolled down Bianca's cheeks. She sniffled for a few moments, and after some reflection, she told the detectives she wanted to talk with her brother alone. Drew and Li agreed, feeling like the young woman was on the verge of making the right decision.

Frank had gone out to the front porch while the detectives were talking to his sister. They went out to the porch, told him Bianca wanted to talk to him, and sent him back inside. They awaited developments on the porch.

A few minutes later, Bianca came to the door, holding the infant, with Frank carrying the toddler.

"Okay," Bianca said to the detectives. "John is living at the Fountainhead Motel on Collins Avenue, room number forty-one. He does handyman work for the motel owner in return for part of the rent. He's registered under the name of John Wilson. John dyed his hair and beard black, and he keeps his car parked at the Standard gas station two blocks from the motel. He repainted it black when we were in Montana."

"Thank you, Bianca," Drew said.

"You did the right thing, Bianca," Li added, "even if it doesn't feel that way right now. I know you saved yourself a lot of grief."

Bianca nodded, turned away, and went back to the living room.

Frank Schumer fished the keys to the rental out of his pocket and handed them to Drew.

"You going to be okay here for a little while?" Drew asked. "We need you to make sure your sister doesn't have second thoughts and doesn't call to warn Watson before we get there."

"Yes, I'm going to stay for a while, anyway," Frank said. "Bianca has agreed to go back home with me, but she won't leave without giving Aubrey a day or two to find someone else to help her with the kids."

"Okay," Drew said. "We appreciate your help, Frank. If you need anything, call us."

"Thanks, I will. But I think we're okay now."

Drew nodded and shook Frank's hand. "Take care of yourself, Frank. See you around."

The detectives hurried out to Tracy's car and Drew hurriedly filled him in.

"Damn, I was hoping to get in on the arrest," Tracy said. "But that motel isn't in my jurisdiction. Do you have Liz's phone number?"

"We do," Li said.

Tracy nodded. "She never leaves work before five. Call her and she can round up some uniformed officers to go along."

"We appreciate your help, Detective Tracy," Drew said. "If you ever get out to LA, you have our numbers."

Tracy smiled. "Yeah, if I'm ever out that way, I'll look you guys up. Good hunting and take care."

"Be safe," Drew said, and he and Li hurried to the rental car.

Chapter Twenty-Two

DREW DROVE BACK TO Surfside while Li called Detective Liz Tracy. Drew knew the Fountainhead Motel was in the heart of Surfside on Collins Avenue. When they have visited the realty office, he had noticed the sign out front further up the street. Li disconnected the call.

"She is waiting for us at the station and will round up some patrol guys to go with us," she said.

About twenty minutes later, Drew and Li were back at the Surfside Police Department on Harding Avenue. Detective Tracy and another Surfside detective, along with eight patrol officers, were waiting for them in the parking lot.

"I did some background work on the Fountainhead Motel," Tracy told them when they got out of the car. "It's an older two-story building on the ocean side of Collins Avenue, and it's currently closed for renovation. Room forty-one is on the second level, just off an outside lobby. The room will be clearly visible from the west side of Collins Avenue. I know a suitable spot there with great site lines."

"Good work," said Drew. "Watson knows both of us. Do you have a pair of binoculars I can use to get eyes on him before we move in?"

"Yes, I've got a pair in my car. What do you think we're looking at?"

"From our experience with him, I don't think John Watson is the type to go down guns blazing. But he might try to run if he thinks he has the opportunity."

"How do you want to handle it?"

"Have your uniformed guys secure the area around the motel," Drew said. "You know the setup better than we do, so use your best judgement. After we get in position at the spot with the good sight lines you mentioned, you and the detective here can roam up and down the street in front of the motel, keeping an eye out for him since he's never seen either of you. If you have an extra radio you can lend us, we can all stay in communication as things develop."

"Yes, I can do that. And this is Detective Mark Epstein, by the way."

Drew and Li shook hands with Epstein, who also looked like a solid cop. Then the LAPD detectives took out their phones and showed Watson's photo to all the Surfside officers.

"According to the witness we spoke with today, Watson has dyed his hair and beard black and he registered at the motel under the alias John Wilson. Also, if he runs, he has a black vehicle parked at a Standard gas station two blocks from the motel."

"Yes, we know where that is," Tracy said. "If he flees on foot, we'll get a unit over there to make sure he doesn't get to the vehicle."

"Then I guess we're ready," Drew said. "We might be in for a long night."

"Not a problem," Tracy said. "You guys want to leave your rental here and ride over with me? I'll drop you at the observation point across the street. Then Mark and I will walk across to the motel side."

"Sounds good," Li said.

"Great. Let me grab a spare radio."

After Detective Tracy returned with the portable radio and handed it to Li, the officers did a communications check. The marked units left first, and split up so half would approach the motel from the north and half from the south. After turning onto Collins Avenue, Tracy pulled her unit into the only available off-street spot on the west side of Collins. Then she pointed out the surveillance location she had told Drew and Li about. The two LAPD detectives headed there while Tracy and Epstein walked towards the motel.

Drew found the location offered the promised excellent site lines with concealment for him and Li. With the binoculars, he had a perfect view of the door of room forty-one across the four-lane street. After a few minutes, he and Li heard the patrol officers notifying Detective Tracy one by one that they were in position. Drew watched the two Surfside detectives making their first pass in front of the motel on foot.

Things went down quicker than Drew had expected. Not five minutes after the cops set up, John Watson appeared n the doorway of room forty-one wearing a pair of paint-stained, dirty denim coveralls without a shirt. He looked like he had recently finished work. He had altered his appearance. Watson had dyed his hair and scruffy beard black, and his hair was longer than the last time Drew had seen him. But Drew, peering through the binoculars, recognized the man immediately.

Watson walked next door and entered the open door of the neighboring room. Drew and Li could hear loud music coming from the room through the wide-open door and assumed a small party was in progress. Li used the radio to notify the Surfside officers they had eyes on the suspect and told them to hold fast.

A few minutes later, Watson exited the room with a beer bottle in his hand and returned to his room. He left his door wide open too, an apparent attempt to catch the cool evening breeze. Li notified the others the suspect had returned to room forty-one and that she and Drew were moving to the room.

Ten minutes later, with Surfside officers securing the stairways up to the second level on the north and south, Drew and Li climbed the south stairway while Tracy and Epstein climbed the north stairway. They met on the second level, on opposite sides of the open doorway. Drew took a standard barricade position against the door frame with his Glock leveled at Watson as he lay on his bed.

Watson glanced at Drew with a brief look of surprise until he recognized the detective. Drew ordered Watson to get off the bed and to walk backwards toward the door with his fingers interlaced and hands on the back of his head. Watson complied. When he approached the door, Drew ordered him to stop and to get on his knees. After Watson again complied, Drew holstered and handcuffed Watson behind his back while Li covered. Watson offered no resistance. Drew stood him up and patted him down, finding no weapons.

"I wondered when you would show up," Watson said, feigning bravado. "What took you so long?"

"John Watson, you're under arrest and have the right to remain silent," Drew said. "I suggest you take advantage of the right." Watson chuckled.

The detectives checked the room, finding empty food containers everywhere, clothes strewn about in piles, rotting uneaten food on paper plates, and other assorted trash throughout. The room reeked of rotting garbage.

Watson's carefree attitude changed abruptly to sullen once he realized that the Los Angeles detectives were a little more business-like this time around.

Drew and Li walked him downstairs and put him in the backseat of Detective Tracy's unmarked car. Epstein caught a ride back to the station with one of the patrol units. Li got in the front seat with Tracy and Drew got in the backseat with Watson and Tracy drove them to the Dade County detention facility. On arrival, Tracy booked Watson on the California grand larceny and receiving stolen property felony warrants.

The arrest and booking had gone down with no problems. But Drew and Li resigned themselves to spending a while longer in Florida until the extradition process ran its course. Both expected Watson would fight extradition back to California.

Chapter Twenty-Three

DREW AND LI HADN'T expected the extradition hearing to get underway until the following Monday, so it surprised them when a judge at the Dade County courthouse set the hearing for Saturday morning to save everyone time and unwanted press coverage.

The Los Angeles detectives watched with interest as the court recognized a deputy public defender as Watson's defense counsel. The lawyer had managed to get a dress shirt and a pair of slacks from somewhere for his new client. Drew and Li were in for another surprise. The public defender addressed the court, stating John Watson waived extradition. They would soon be on their way back home.

Sunday morning, Drew and Li picked up Watson from the detention facility and drove him in their rental car to the Miami International airport. Watson was loose and talkative, even a little flippant. While Drew had advised him of his constitutional rights, Watson waived them and told the LA cops he had nothing to do with the Wonderland killings. He stated that Tony Dunn had been behind all of it. Drew asked no followup questions, having no intention of interviewing Watson in the backseat of a rental car or during the flight back to Los Angeles. Instead, he was eager to get Watson into an interview room where he could interrogate him properly this time. However, he and Li would keep their ears open for any incriminating statements Watson might make on the trip home.

The American Airlines flight touched down at LAX at eleven fifty-two, Los Angeles time, after an uneventful flight. Drew had called ahead to Estrada before leaving Miami and felt confident his teammate would have a handle on things when they landed. Drew had seen the Miami papers before boarding the plane and knew it had angered the local reporters that they hadn't learned about the arrest of John Watson until he was beyond their reach. He knew the Los Angeles paparazzi would be impatiently awaiting their arrival in force.

Once the plane had taxied to the jetway, a flight attendant approached Drew and Li. She asked them to stay seated while the other passengers deplaned and informed them that LAPD officers were waiting for them on the tarmac with security and a transport vehicle. Drew smiled, knowing Estrada and Moreno had come through for him. They would foil the press once again.

After the other passengers had exited the plane, Drew and Li took Watson down the exterior stairway attached to the jetway. They put Watson in the backseat of an unmarked unit driven by Estrada. Once again, Drew got in the backseat with the prisoner and Li got in front with Estrada. Forty-five minutes later, the detectives put Watson in an elevator and took him up to the fifth floor of the PAB. There, they ushered him straight into an interview room.

Drew and Estrada would handle the interview. Li would observe the interview from behind the one-way glass, along with Lieutenant Moreno and Los Angeles County Deputy District Attorney Alex Douglas, the prosecutor who had taken part in the LASD warrant service on Tony Dunn's home. The DA had appointed Douglas to prosecute all cases against Tony Dunn, which included all cases associated with the Wonderland murders.

After removing the handcuffs from John Watson, Drew reminded him he had advised him of his Miranda rights. Then he had Watson sign a written statement to that effect. At first, Watson agreed to waive his rights and talk with the detectives. Again, he admitted he had left the front door to the Wonderland house unlocked for the killers, and only because Tony Dunn forced him to do it. But he denied he had anything to do with the murders and that Tony Dunn had responsibility for all of it.

"Was Tony Dunn at the house during the murders?" Drew asked.

"Get serious, Detective. Tony doesn't get his own hands dirty. He hires people to do his dirty work."

"You claim you had nothing to do with the murders besides leaving the door unlocked," Drew said. "Who did you let into the house?"

"I never saw them," Watson said. "Like I told the other detectives. I unlocked the door and I split. I wasn't there when they went in."

"You're lying, asshole," Estrada said, pointing his finger at Watson. "We got your prints from the scene."

"I don't doubt that, Detective," Watson smirked. "I did business with the Wonderland crew and spent a lot of time there. My fingerprints were probably all over the house. But I wasn't there when the murders went down."

Watson didn't know about the bloody handprint recovered from the bed railing in Joe Allen's bedroom. But the detectives weren't about to give away that detail. Instead, Drew turned the conversation back to Tony Dunn.

"Okay, Watson, you said Tony Dunn ordered the murders. Tell us what you know about it. Who do you think he sent to the house to do the murders?"

"I'm not saying anymore about Tony Dunn," Watson said. "If he found out I rolled over on him, he would kill me and my family."

"Tell me this, Watson," Estrada said. "You said Dunn forced you to leave the door of the Wonderland house unlocked for his crew."

"That's right. Dunn threatened to kill me if I refused to go along with it. I didn't want any part of it, but I had no choice."

"And then you unlocked the door and split, right?" Estrada asked.

"That's right."

Drew took over. "You split because you knew what was going to happen. Isn't that right?"

"Okay, Detective. Sure, I had some idea about why Dunn wanted me to leave the door unlocked. But I didn't know they were going to kill everyone in the house."

"John, we can put you inside that house at the time of the murder," Drew said. "The only way you're getting your neck out of the noose is helping us prove Tony Dunn ordered the murders."

"Can't do it, Detective," Watson said, shaking his head. "I think I've said enough. I want a lawyer."

Watson had said the magic words. The detectives couldn't continue the interview once the suspect invoked his right to have an attorney present until he got representation.

"Wait here," Drew said to Watson. Then he and Estrada left the room and shut the door. They met Li, Moreno and the deputy DA in the corridor.

"What do you think?" Drew asked Alex Douglas.

"He admitted to unlocking the door and knowing someone would get killed," Douglas said. "He's part of the conspiracy and admitted it even if he didn't take part in the killings. His claim of coercion isn't a defense under California law. We have the bloody handprint, but we don't even have to prove he took part in the murders. I think we have a strong case."

"So we arrest and charge him?" Drew asked.

"Yes," Douglas said. "We will have to convict Watson before there will be any possibility of him rolling over on Dunn and identifying the actual killers."

"I agree," Drew said. He turned to Estrada. "Let's do it." The detectives reentered the interview room.

Estrada told Watson to stand and then put the handcuffs back on him.

"John Watson, you're under arrest for the murders of Joe Allen, Harlan Tate, Nancy Poole, and Amanda Quinn," Drew said. "And for the attempted murder of Dawn Allen."

Watson made no reply. From his expression, Drew thought the man had finally realized just how much trouble he was actually in.

Following his arrest, the detectives transported John Watson to Men's Central Jail on Bauchet and booked him on the murder and attempted murder charges. Deputy DA Douglas filed the four counts of murder and one count of attempted murder.

Chapter Twenty-Four

AT THEIR MONDAY MORNING case meeting, Drew noted they hadn't heard from Dennis Mack recently. He had some questions he wanted to ask Mack after interviewing John Watson. He wanted to know from Dennis Mack how often he had seen Watson at the Wonderland house before the murders and whether Mack knew whether Watson had ever been inside Joe Allen's bedroom while visiting the house. Drew and Li had to go to the district attorney's office on another case, so Oscar Estrada volunteered to run Mack down and get the answers to Drew's questions.

Estrada called Tiny Tim to chat about Mack. Tim told him Mack was staying over on Yucca Street in Hollywood with a new girlfriend. He said Mack didn't have a phone, and he didn't know the girlfriend's number, but he gave Estrada the address.

Estrada grabbed Roy Hutchinson, another Homicide Special detective, to back him up, and they drove over to the address Tiny Tim had given him. When they arrived on Yucca Street in central Hollywood, they found it was an older, dilapidated apartment building. Oscar knocked on the door of the apartment number Tim had given him. He announced himself and called out to Mack by his first name. The detectives heard someone approach the door. It was Mack.

"How do I know you dudes are really cops?"

"Hey David, it's me, Estrada," Oscar said. "I have a couple of questions for you."

There was a moment of silence on the other side of the door, and then the detectives heard the crashing of furniture, running feet, and a slamming door.

Estrada looked at Hutchinson. "That asshole is running!"

They ran to the rear of the apartment building, and as they rounded a corner, Oscar nearly ran right into Mack, coming from the opposite direction. Estrada knocked Mack to the ground. Hutchinson kneeled on him and hooked him up with his handcuffs. Estrada helped Mack to his feet.

"What the fuck were you doing, Dennis?" he growled.

Mack, clearly stoned, slurred his speech when he answered. "Hey, man. I thought somebody was after me."

"Yeah. It was us. But we just want to talk."

Mack was coming down from his last fix. He muttered, "Yeah, man. I'm sorry."

Estrada and Hutchinson put Mack in the backseat of their car and drove him back to the PAB and put him in an interview room. Mack was drowsy and Hutchinson went to get him a cup of coffee.

Estrada asked Mack about Watson. "Hey, Dennis. Was John Watson at the Wonderland house often?"

"Yeah, dude. Like every day."

"Did you ever see him go into Allen's bedroom?"

"Are you shitting me?" Mack said. Joe's room? "No fucking way. Joe would have killed that punk bastard."

"Did Watson have the free run of the house?"

"No way, man!"

"Why not?" Hutchinson asked, having just walked back into the room with the coffee for Mack.

"Because Watson was a thief. He was always bringing stolen shit over to trade for dope. Watson stole from everyone, including his friends. He was a strung-out dude. Allen and Tate were running a dope business and couldn't afford to have Watson around stealing them blind. They didn't trust him. That's why Harlan got pissed at Nancy when he found out she had given him a key to the house."

Mack was still groggy, but after drinking the coffee, he was coherent. "Hey, I heard from someone a couple of dudes had come to the house looking for Allen and found the bodies. They helped themselves to whatever was left in the house."

"Do you know their names?" Estrada asked.

"A dude called Stretch and one called Smokey from Sacto. That's all I heard. They were down to take Joe up north for a court appearance."

Estrada remembered hearing the names and the same story when he and Drew had interviewed Bob Farmer.

"Do you know a guy named Jack Langley?"

"Yeah, I know him. Tiny Tim also knows him."

"Do you think Langley could have been involved in the murders?"

Mack laughed. "No way, man. Langley acted like he was in the mob. He tried to impress people with his big-time connections that didn't even exist. He also traded in stolen property. Langley is more bullshit and bark than bite."

Having asked Mack all the questions he could think of, Mack called Tiny Tim Johnson to come to the PAB to pick Mack up.

Later, after checking several sources, including moniker files and shake cards, Estrada identified "Stretch" as James Baker and "Smokey" as Charles Crampton. More background checking led him to LAPD Valley financial crimes detectives in Van Nuys. The Valley unit had both men in custody on forgery charges. Estrada waited until Drew returned to see if he thought it worthwhile to go to the Van Nuys jail to interview Baker and Crampton.

When Drew and Li returned from the district attorney's office, Estrada told him about the interview with Dennis Mack and that Mack had mentioned the same two guys Bob Farmer had told them about, Stretch and Smokey.

"Yeah, I remember," Drew said. "The two guys Farmer said went to the Wonderland house after the murders."

"That's right. I did some background checking and identified them as James Baker and Charles Crampton. Valley has them both in jail in Van Nuys on forgery charges."

"Let's take a run to Van Nuys and see what they have to say," Drew said. Leaving Li at the office, Drew and Estrada headed for the Van Nuys station.

James Baker told the detectives he and Crampton went to the Wonderland house to pick up Joe Allen and drive him to court in Sacramento because Allen didn't have reliable transportation.

"When we got there, we found the front door ajar," Baker said. "Then when we went inside, we found the bodies. Man, it was a bad scene, blood all over the place."

Baker proved remarkably candid. He told Drew and Estrada that when they checked the bedrooms, he had stepped over the body of Dawn Allen and heard her moan.

"Why didn't you do something?" Drew asked. "Like calling nine-one-one."

"She was in a bad way," Baker said. "I figured she was going to die anyway." Baker made a pathetic attempt to justify his lack of action. "Why attract attention, right?"

"She lived," Drew said, not bothering to hide his disdain for Baker. "She was alone on the floor in pain for hours more after you left."

"Well, look, I told a neighbor we ran into on the way out of the house about the bodies. I figured he would call the cops."

Drew just shook his head.

After they finished with Baker, the detectives asked to see Crampton, but he declined their invitation for an interview. It didn't bother Drew or Estrada. They had already concluded that Baker and Crampton had only been a pair of scavengers and neither could tell them anything useful about the murders.

Chapter Twenty-Five

THE LASD NARCOTICS Bureau had stayed on top of Tony Dunn ever since they had served the no-knock warrant at his residence. They had identified another Dunn associate through an informant and their surveillance activities. A deputy with the narcotics unit called Drew and passed on the information.

The narcotics bureau deputies had observed Regina "Gina" Ramsey moving to and from Dunn's residence regularly. Her husband, former bail bondsman Terry Ramsey, was a longtime Dunn business acquaintance. He had recently gained release from federal prison in Lompoc, California, after completing his sentence after being convicted of attempting to bribe a federal magistrate on Tony Dunn's behalf.

Terry Ramsey's wife, Gina, had been in an ongoing and close relationship with Tony Dunn while he served his sentence. Gina and Dunn's relationship wasn't about business. She had an addiction to cocaine.

Terry had accused her of looting his bail bond business during his incarceration and was pursuing legal action against her through the district attorney's office. He had discovered a substantial amount of cash missing when released from federal prison. So far, no arrests or prosecutions had resulted.

By the time Terry got out of jail, Gina had ended her relationship with Dunn and had hooked up with a biker out of Bakersfield. Terry had become her ex-husband. Drew and Li wanted to go to Bakersfield to talk to Gina Ramsey to see what she could tell them about Tony Dunn, since their relationship had been going on during the time of the Wonderland murders.

Drew phoned Gina, and she agreed to meet with the detectives, but only at the Bakersfield Police Department. It seemed she didn't trust the LAPD. Drew figured the lack of trust stemmed from the influence of Tony Dunn. He had probably told her about all the bent cops on his payroll.

The day after phoning her, Drew and Li met with her in Bakersfield. She shared her addiction problems with the detectives. Gina Ramsey was a nervous, mousy blonde who claimed she had checked her addiction and was determined to stay clean. She clearly hated Dunn, describing him as the most evil person she had ever known. But she denied knowing anything about Dunn's home robbery or any involvement he may have had in the Wonderland murders. But she told the detectives one thing they found interesting.

"I had a late breakfast with John Watson the morning of July first," she said. "We met at Tiny Naylor's restaurant on the corner of Ventura and Laurel Canyon Boulevards in Studio City."

Drew and Li knew that was only a mile or two down Laurel Canyon from Dunn's place, and if Gina's story was true, the late breakfast would have been after the murders, but before authorities had discovered the bodies.

"John seemed extremely nervous and shook up," Ramsey said. "I'd never seen him like that before."

"Did he tell you what he was nervous about?" Drew asked.

Ramsey shook her head. "No, he shared nothing with me at all."

Drew confronted Gina with a rumor he knew was floating around.

"Did Tony have you drive the killers to Wonderland in your car the morning of the murders?"

"What? No! I did no such thing and Tony never asked me to do anything like that."

The detectives had no evidence of her involvement or participation in the murders. But several sources had told them about the rumor. Drew and Li thought Gina Ramsey was cooperative, but they both also believed she knew more than she let on. They assumed she feared repercussions if she told them anything about Tony Dunn, and he found out about it.

"Thanks for taking the time to talk with us," Drew said. "We might circle back to you if we have any further questions."

After Gina left the station, Drew and Li got back in the car and drove back to Los Angeles.

While Drew and Li were in Bakersfield, Estrada returned to Cedars-Sinai to spend more time with Dawn Allen, whose condition continued to improve. Estrada believed the more time he spent with Dawn, the more her trust and confidence in him would grow. While Dawn seemed to cooperate, Estrada believed she was holding back information about her husband, Joe, and perhaps key elements pertaining to the murders. He understood her reluctance to cooperate fully, but the detectives still had many more questions they hoped Dawn could answer.

Did she know details about the motive of the attack? Did she recall anything more about John Watson and his activities around the time of the murders? Could she identify any of the suspects or provide descriptions of them? What specifics about the goings on at the Wonderland house had her husband shared with her prior to his death? Who else might the investigators talk to? Estrada was determined to be patient and let things play out, staying hopeful that Dawn would eventually fill in some of the missing pieces in the investigation.

Sometimes, when he asked her about Joe, Dawn Allen appeared guarded and even defensive about discussing her late husband and his activities. And it seemed strange to Estrada that Dawn didn't seem to mourn Joe's death or the deaths of the others at the Wonderland house. She always boasted about what a badass Joe had been, but exhibited no grief over his death. He just hoped at some point, Dawn would open up to him.

Chapter Twenty-Six

THE DRUG BUSINESS AT Tony Dunn's place had not slowed. Patrons were coming and going at all hours and it seemed the only thing that Dunn could have done to generate more business would have been the installation of a twenty-four-hour drive-through window alongside his home. Dunn seemed unconcerned that half of the narcotics cops in Los Angeles County were watching.

Not to be outdone by the Los Angeles County Sheriff's Department Narcotics Bureau, the LAPD Narcotics Division ramped up surveillance on Dunn's home and several of his clubs as well. Narcotics detectives were busy putting together a damning affidavit defining their observations, witness statements, and informant information. This time it was the LAPD who obtained a no-knock warrant. And once again, Drew and his team received an invitation to the party. Making drug cases against Dunn would not get Drew what he really wanted. Murder charges filed on Tony Dunn. But he was happy enough about the LAPD and other agencies keeping the pressure on Dunn and his illegal business activities.

The LAPD had set up their command post in the same spot used by the LASD Narcotics Bureau months before. It was off Berry Drive, a secluded residential street just off Laurel Canyon Boulevard and down the hill from Dunn's home. Drew, Li, and Estrada arrived there at just before dawn. The SWAT team was busy double-checking their weapons and gear. It didn't surprise Drew to learn Blake Lawrence, a local newspaper reporter, was also there, double-checking his pen and notepad.

Lieutenant Ron Griffith, the field commander for the SWAT unit, had been an LAPD academy classmate of Estrada's. Griffith and Estrada had contended for the top shooter honors in their class, and Griffith had beaten Estrada out by only a few points.

Griffith was concerned about having a reporter at the scene, but Estrada assured him it wouldn't be a problem. Blake Lawrence had no interest in SWAT tactics. It was Dunn he wished to exploit. Rogers still wasn't happy about it. SWAT priorities differed from those of homicide cops intending to leverage the press on the sly to help put a murder case together. Estrada had invited Blake Lawrence to cover the warrant service after sharing his idea with Drew and Li.

Lieutenant Griffith had consulted with his LASD Special Enforcement Bureau counterpart and his operation would mirror the SEB operation. Just before first light, SWAT officers would proceed up the hill, deploy around the perimeter of the house, and then a breaching team would initiate the operation at the front door. When the front door went down and the flash-bang grenade detonated, the other breach teams would force entry at their designated windows and sliding glass doors.

As the sun rose above the hills, the flash-bang grenade exploded. The front door went down, and the SWAT officers smashed in every first-floor window and glass sliding door in the house, followed immediately with heavily armed cops entering the house from multiple points. When Lieutenant Griffith announced the scene was secure over the radio, Drew, Li, and Estrada hurried up the hill to the house with the newspaper reporter in tow.

Unlike the previous raid, Dunn's bodyguard, Justin Carr, hadn't even got out of bed, much less offered resistance when the SWAT officers poured through his bedroom window. The cops found no firearms in the room, only a broken pool cue. Other officers dragged Dunn from his bed, and just like before, he was mad as hell.

The homicide detectives arrived just in time to hear Tony Dunn's protests.

"Why me again?" blustered one of the biggest cocaine dealers in Southern California. "Why?"

Drew answered him, further enraging the gangster. "It's against the law to deal coke in California, Tony. You keep doing it and we will keep serving search warrants."

"I'm sick of looking at your face," Dunn retorted. "You keep pushing me because you can't frame me for your murders. Something could happen to you, Detective."

"Is that a threat, Mr. Dunn?" Li asked. "I'd be happy to put another charge on you."

Before he could answer, the narcotics detectives escorted Dunn to his now legendary safe in his bedroom. Dunn opened it reluctantly. The detectives removed bundles of cash and over two pounds of powder cocaine. Apparently, Dunn's suppliers had recently delivered it just in time for the New Year celebrations.

The Homicide Special Section detectives enjoyed the thought that Dunn would believe he had a snitch in his midst after getting hit immediately after receiving a large shipment. Drug dealers didn't really believe in such coincidences.

As the SWAT officers frog marched Dunn and Carr out the front door in handcuffs, the media met them with their digital cameras and video cameras recording it all. SWAT commander Griffith didn't understand or care for that part. But Drew, Li, and Estrada knew having Tony Dunn on the front page of the *Times* and on television news in handcuffs did more for the murder investigation than keeping the press away.

Deputy District Attorney Alex Douglas was also present. He was staying close to any law enforcement activity involving Tony Dunn. He intended to file every criminal charge against Dunn he could justify in his attempt to rid Los Angeles County of one well-entrenched, drug-dealing gangster.

The feds had indicted Dunn on arson and racketeering charges, and the trial was about to start. Some rival drug dealers had robbed and humiliated him. The police were slamming him with no-knock search warrants and he faced multiple state narcotics distribution and possession charges. Multiple law enforcement agencies were constantly following or surveilling him, and Homicide Special was investigating him as a suspect in a quadruple murder. Some might say Dunn had a full plate.

Chapter Twenty-Seven

THE PLAN ALL ALONG was to use his indictment for murder and attempted murder to pressure John Watson into testifying again Dunn and the actual killers. The district attorney's office wanted Watson to feel trapped inside a box with no way out. Now, with Watson behind bars and facing an uncertain future, the investigators and the prosecutor felt it was time to see if their plan would work. Drew and his team also felt it was time to shake things up to let certain people know they weren't going away.

The team's next target was Justin Carr, Dunn's bodyguard. Carr had to believe a weasel like John Watson facing a trial on four counts of murder and one count of attempted murder would do anything to save his own skin. It was maybe the one time the detectives could test their theory by putting pressure on Carr.

With the backing of the deputy DA handling the Wonderland cases, the team would arrest Carr and book him into jail on the same four charges of murder and one charge of attempted murder. The theory was that would pit the men against each other, with Watson and Carr competing to be the first to strike a deal to avoid life imprisonment by agreeing to testify against the other. They also thought it possible that Carr might testify against Dunn to save himself.

Another consideration was that with both Watson and Carr in jail, realizing the possibility that one or both might talk to the cops and district attorney, Nash might decide it was time to head straight to Los Angeles International Airport to take his leave. To prevent that possibility, the investigators would use the Special Investigation Section (SIS), the elite tactical detective and surveillance unit of the Los Angeles Police Department, organized under the Robbery–Homicide Division, to keep tabs on Dunn to prevent him from ducking out of the country.

An attempt by Dunn to make a hasty departure right after the arrests of Watson and Carr for the Wonderland murders would make him look guilty.

It was all a crapshoot, but the detectives were running out of options. They hadn't located a single witness willing to testify that Tony Dunn had ordered the killings, even though Drew, LI, and Estrada felt certain he had.

The Homicide Special team and Deputy District Attorney Alex Douglas felt they had a strong case against John Watson if they ultimately had to prosecute him for the murders and the attempted murder of Dawn Allen. But Justin Carr was a different story. Carr worked for Dunn as a bouncer at Dunn's club on Sunset Boulevard and as Dunn's enforcer and bodyguard. While the cops and prosecutor felt certain that Carr had not only been involved but had actually taken part in the murders, they couldn't prove it.

Arresting Carr was only an attempt to bluff him into cooperating. They could make a probable cause arrest, but the jail would have to kick him after seventy-two hours if the deputy DA didn't file charges, and he had no intention of filing charges on Carr in connection with the Wonderland murders with no substantial evidence.

If they couldn't turn Carr and get him to roll on Watson or Dunn, the district attorney was ready to file the felony assault charge on Carr he had been holding back regarding the LASD warrant service the previous July when Carr had fired on SEB deputies. They figured Dunn would post Carr's bail if it came to that, in which case the detectives would gain nothing, but lose nothing by making the arrest. If nothing else, by shaking things up, they would have key players looking over their shoulders, waiting for the other shoe to drop.

The detectives wanted to nail Carr on the street when he left the club. They would have SIS already set up on Dunn at his home. They would arrest Carr in two days during the early morning hours on Friday. That way, the detectives would have access to him over a long weekend before the deputy DA would have to file the felony assault charge on Monday to hold him. If it came to that.

Drew and Estrada were in Drew's city ride outside the Fiction club on Sunset Boulevard when the club closed at two in the morning. They had spotted Carr standing outside the front doors several times since arriving and had verified his car was in the small employee's lot. Two marked Hollywood Division units waited on side streets on either side of the club, covering both directions, ready to initiate a felony traffic stop as soon as Carr pulled out of the lot.

Five minutes after two, Carr's vehicle exited the lot and the marked units pulled Carr over on Sunset Boulevard, four blocks from the club. After the textbook felony stop, the patrol officers had Carr handcuffed in the back of one of the black and white units on the way to lock up at Hollywood Station.

Drew and Estrada had watched the stop and the arrest but had hung back. They had already coordinated with the patrol guys in advance and followed the transport vehicle to the station. After the arresting officers had booked Carr, Drew had the jail staff to put Carr in an interview room. And then the detectives walked in and sat down at the table across from Carr. Drew reintroduced himself and Estrada.

"I know who you are," Carr said. "This is bullshit."

"Is it?" Drew asked. "I guess you know we arrested John Watson, and he's talking to us. Why do you think we arrested you? We know you were at the Wonderland house during the murders."

"You don't know shit," Carr growled.

Drew ignored the remark. "Watson hasn't cut a deal with the DA yet," he said. "But it's only a matter of time. We know you took part in the murders, so there will be no immunity offer. But you could save yourself from a life sentence if you cut a deal before Watson does. The clock is ticking. The DA is only offering one deal."

"Fuck off," Carr said. "I want a lawyer. I'm not talking to you."

Drew and Estrada realized two things. Dunn had already schooled Carr on what to say to the cops. Nothing. And the second thing was Carr hated cops, Drew and Estrada in particular.

"We're going to hang the Wonderland murders around your neck," Estrada said. "You better think about whether you really want to take the weight for your boss while you're sitting in jail."

Carr glared at him but said nothing in reply. It was clear the threat hadn't impressed him. The detectives ended the interview and told the jail staff they could put Carr in a cell.

Ten minutes after Drew and Estrada left Hollywood Station, Drew's phone rang. It was a member of SIS who told him Dunn was on the move. SIS had followed him to a house in the Hollywood Hills. It was a new location from which another Dunn associate had emerged. The SIS officer told Drew that Dunn had attempted to conceal his vehicle out of apparent concern over the recent activities and was keeping a low profile. Drew ended the call.

"I guess Carr got his phone call after we left," Drew said. "Dunn left home and went to the house of an associate in the Hollywood Hills."

"Whose house?" Estrada asked.

"Don't know yet," Drew said. "I got the address from SIS and I'll look it up when we get back to the PAB."

"We will not turn Carr," Estrada said.

"No," Drew agreed. "That part of the plan is dead. We will have to come up with another strategy. Maybe work on Watson."

"We could try using the same tactic we used with Carr," Estrada said. "But I'm not feeling optimistic. Watson is bound to know Carr even better than we do. He probably knows Carr won't roll on Dunn."

"Nothing ventured, nothing gained," Drew said.

Chapter Twenty-Eight

AHEAD OF THE EXPIRATION of the seventy-two hour hold on Justin Carr, Deputy District Attorney Alex Douglas filed the felony assault charge and Carr appeared for his arraignment before a judge at the Clara Shortridge Foltz Criminal Justice Center on the Monday morning after his arrest. The judge bound Carr over for trial, set a March court date, and released him on bail. Drew and his team hadn't bothered to attend the proceeding, having lost in interest in Carr when it became clear he wouldn't cooperate. They were at their desks at the PAB on Monday morning when they received the first of two unexpected visitors.

The first was a man named Bill Burgess, a senior arson investigator for the Los Angeles City Fire Department. He revealed he worked for the US Attorney's District Organized Crime Strike Force, which comprised several law enforcement agencies, including federal prosecutors, the FBI, the Bureau of Alcohol, Tobacco and Firearms, the IRS and the Los Angeles City Fire Department Arson Unit. The strike force had indicted Tony Dunn and several associates on arson-for-hire and racketeering charges and the trial was about the begin.

"I know you guys are looking at Tony Dunn in connection with your murder investigation," Burgess told the investigators. "Not sure if you can use my information, but I thought I'd stop by and talk to you anyway."

"We're happy to listen," Drew said, "although I'm unsure how Dunn's federal case could relate to our investigation."

"There is probably no direct relationship," Burgess said. "I just thought you might want to know we've learned that Dunn has a considerable number of influential people, political and law enforcement types, running interference for him."

"Okay, tell us what you know," Drew said, suddenly interested in hearing something that might confirm what he already suspected about Dunn having corrupt officials providing cover for him and his illegal business activities.

"Last year, the mayor appointed Zachary Fleming the president of the Los Angeles Fire Commission, which oversees the Los Angeles City Fire Department. The commission calls all the shots regarding department resources, policy, and general oversight. In short, they run the entire show."

"And the appointment of this Zachary Fleming as president of the commission is something you see as a problem?" Drew asked.

"You could say that," Burgess said. "Fleming is a Burbank attorney, and not just any attorney. He represents Tony Dunn and will defend him in the federal trial that starts next week. Before Fleming's appointment, we had been pursuing Tony Dunn on several allegations of arson for hire. As soon as Fleming took office, my unit's superiors told us to stop focusing our investigation on Dunn and to stop pursuing him independently."

"If I'm understanding you correctly, you're saying your boss is Tony Dunn's attorney," Drew said.

"Exactly right. That's a big problem, and it is far more than just a conflict of interest. Fleming is literally preventing my unit from investigating his client. And weirdly, it's absolutely legal because he has the mayor's backing."

"Well, at least the feds got involved," Estrada said. "Maybe they will get a conviction."

Burgess shook his head. "I'm afraid the corruption goes far beyond city government officials. It's likely Dunn has also bought influence with some of the strike force people. I think it's a much larger conspiracy. I don't feel confident the feds will get a conviction."

It seemed clear to Drew that Burgess was a professional who took pride in what he did, and the man felt frustrated over the improprieties that interfered with his unit's investigations. Drew felt empathy for the man, but saw no link between Dunn's obvious connection with arson for hire and his murder investigation. Still, he appreciated Burgess had confirmed that Dunn enjoyed considerable influence among many individuals holding powerful political positions in Los Angeles. It probably explained why Captain Meyers had forbidden him from hauling Dunn in for interrogation and had warned him not to harass Dunn. Drew suspected the corruption went far above the head of the Robbery-Homicide Division.

Drew thanked Burgess for the information and told him he would stay alert for any interference with his own investigation of Dunn in connection with his team's murder case.

After Burgess left the office, Estrada said, "It might be worthwhile to sit in the courtroom during that federal trial. Just to see if we see signs of corruption."

"I agree," Drew said.

"If nothing else, it's a chance to give Dunn another poke in the eye if we make sure he sees us sitting in the courtroom," Li snickered.

Drew chuckled. "Yeah, there is that."

The team had been back at their office for about an hour after taking a break for lunch when their second unexpected visitor walked in. He too, coincidentally, was part of the US Attorney's District Organized Crime Strike Force who had investigated Tony Dunn, and identified himself as Jim Kemp, the supervising agent for the Bureau of Alcohol, Tobacco, and Firearms contingent on loan to the strike force.

Kemp came on like a slick operator with a good old boy southern drawl. He was tall at about six feet four inches with gaunt, hawkish features. Clearly, Kemp felt accustomed to using his size, demeanor, and status as a federal law enforcement agent to intimidate and get away with it.

After the introductions and some small talk, Kemp got down to the reason for his visit. Drew and his team were wary because Kemp didn't behave the way most law enforcement types did when the company of other law enforcement officers. He gave off the vibe that he expected complete cooperation from the locals. And as the LAPD detectives knew from experience, the feds always wanted all the information they could get, with no intention of sharing anything they had in return.

"Because of our investigation, the US Attorney's Office has indicted Anthony Dunn on charges he orchestrated the torching of various businesses in Southern California and Las Vegas," Kemp said. "They also indicted him on other RICO charges. The trial starts next week."

"Yeah, we heard something about it," Drew said, not hiding that Kemp's news hadn't impressed him.

Kemp didn't seem to notice, and pressed on. "Our investigation is ongoing and we are pursuing other suspects and charges against Anthony Dunn. I want all the information you have on Dunn at this point in your investigation."

"Yeah, well, that's not going to happen," Drew said. "We don't release or share any information on an ongoing murder investigation."

Kemp appeared miffed. "Hey, look. I'm just an old country boy who believes in total cooperation between law enforcement agencies. Your cooperation could be crucial in convicting Dunn of additional charges as well as convicting other suspects involved in the conspiracy. We need the LAPD on board."

"Tell you what, Agent Kemp. You guys worry about convicting Tony Dunn on your arson for hire and racketeering charges and we'll worry about solving our murder case. We're not giving up any information on an unsolved murder investigation to anyone unless a court orders us to do so. And even then, it's a stretch to believe we would do it."

Red-faced and open-mouthed, Kemp stared at the detectives for a few moments, and then he turned and stormed out of the office without another word. After listening to his earlier visitor, Bill Burgess, Drew didn't trust Kemp. On top of that, he got bad vibes from the man. If Kemp went over his head and he got pressure from the tenth floor to cooperate, he would only feed Kemp innocuous information.

"I don't think he liked you much," Estrada said to Drew.

"Nope," Li chuckled.

"Screw him," Drew said. "The feds are nothing but trouble."

Chapter Twenty-Nine

THE HOMICIDE SPECIAL investigators skipped the first few days of Dunn's federal trial, but on the twenty-seventh of January, Drew, Li, and Estrada entered the federal courtroom on the day ATF Agent Kemp would testify. At the crux of the federal case was the assertion Dunn and his three co-defendants were members of an organized arson ring. The government held that the group would purchase businesses at a discount, insure them, pay someone to burn them down, and profit by collecting the insurance settlements.

The detectives arrived early and took seats in the second row behind the bar, the railing separating the courtroom spectators from the participants in a trial. When Dunn turned around to survey the spectators, he spotted the LAPD detectives immediately.

Dunn was in no mood to have the detectives sitting and staring at him during the proceedings. He kept peering back over his shoulder, glaring at the detectives throughout. Drew thought he saw concern in Dunn's stares, but also a great deal of anger. It got worse when Estrada caught Dunn's eye and mouthed a vulgar expression at him. Dunn tried to rise from his chair and his lawyers had to restrain him.

Finally, Agent Kemp took the stand to testify. Curiously, Kemp's testimony appeared to lack directness in implicating Dunn, but was laser-focused when implicating his three co-defendants. Having seen enough, the RHD detectives left the courtroom when Kemp finished and before the prosecution called their next witness.

"For someone claiming he wanting to nail Tony Dunn's hide to the wall, Kemp seemed to pull a lot of the punches aimed at him," Estrada said.

"You think Kemp is dirty?" Li asked.

"All I know," Drew said, "is I feel even better about refusing to cooperate with him. I wouldn't trust Kemp further than I could throw him."

After they left the federal courthouse, Estrada left Drew and Li to drive over to Cedars-Sinai Hospital. The day had finally come for the hospital to release Dawn Allen and to transfer her to Rancho Los Amigos Hospital to work with rehabilitation therapists. Estrada wanted to help her settle into her new environment and to make certain the security arrangements satisfied him. Like her neurologist at Cedars-Sinai, Estrada had grown protective of Dawn Allen.

Drew and Li got in his car to drive to an address in the Hollywood Hills. Drew had consulted property records and learned the name of the owner of the house that SIS had followed Dunn to the night they arrested Justin Carr.

The Mount Olympus section of Los Angeles was an older but high-dollar area in the Hollywood Hills. It was the neighborhood the former bail bondsman Terry Ramsey called home.

Terry had a long rap sheet, and it fit someone involved in organized crime. It included prior convictions for statutory rape and grand theft and later convictions for criminal breach of fiduciary duty, not to mention the prison stint for attempting to bribe a federal judge. Ramsey's application for a bail bond license and his association with Tony Dunn went back to 2002. At that time, Ramsey had managed several nightclubs owned by Dunn, but he apparently did more for Dunn than just manage his clubs.

The California Department of Insurance, the agency regulating the bail bonds business in the state, had revoked Terry Ramsey's bail bond license after a federal court had convicted him for attempting to bribe a federal magistrate and sentenced him to federal prison. Ramsey had tried to bribe the judge to get a more lenient sentence for one of Dunn's drug dealer associates. Rumors were that Ramsey still operated his bail bond business through a fictitious business name filed in Los Angeles County, run by his associates. That business had posted Justin Carr's bail, suggesting that Ramsey was still doing business with Tony Dunn.

Drew was making a planned cold call visit to Ramsey to deny him the chance to prepare when he wasn't expecting the detectives wanted to talk to him. Drew didn't know what to expect, but sometimes cold call visits were interesting and fruitful.

When Drew rang the doorbell, it provoked the barking of more than one dog on the other side of the door. Moments later, they heard a muffled response from Ramsey.

"Who is it?"

"LAPD homicide," Drew shouted, standing to the side of the door with Li behind him.

"Hold on while I put up the dogs," Ramsey called back.

"Appreciate it," Li said to Drew's back.

A few minutes later, a disheveled Terry Ramsey, clad in a T-shirt and baggy sweatpants, opened the door and invited the detectives inside.

Li wrinkled her nose when a stench reminiscent of the Los Angeles Zoo before cage cleaning time in August met the detectives. A quick scan of the living room confirmed the source of the unpleasant odors, numerous piles of dog excrement, some old, and some newer, spread liberally throughout the room. The detectives found the contrast between the feces and the expensive-looking beige carpet striking.

"We're investigating a Laurel Canyon homicide case with four victims that occurred on the first of July last summer," Drew said.

Ramsey offered a half-assed sardonic reply. "You think I did it?"

"Everyone is a suspect until they aren't," Drew replied. "So, yeah, you could be a suspect. We have information suggesting your wife, Gina, while having the affair with Tony Dunn, was involved."

"Ex-wife," Ramsey corrected. "I divorced that bitch."

Ramsey seemed visibly upset with Regina Ramsey for telling the cops she had slept with Tony Dunn while he was serving his sentence in federal prison.

"She looted my business of over two hundred thousand dollars and blew it on coke. Instead of the cops doing their jobs and arresting her for grand theft, you show up here to give me grief and I'm the victim."

Ramsey continued growing more antagonistic and began a profanity-laced rant about his ex-wife and useless cops in general.

Drew and Li both tried to calm him and to get the discussion back around to their investigation, but the man only grew more stirred up.

"Look, I don't give a single fuck about your murder investigation," Ramsey said in no uncertain terms. "That doesn't have shit to do with me."

"Guess you and Tony are still tight," Drew said. "You must be the forgiving type, Terry. We know he spent some time here a few nights ago, and you put up bail for Justin Carr."

"What the fuck?" Ramsey snarled. "You're watching my house and snooping into my business? That's harassment. Get the fuck out of my house."

The detectives turned and walked to the front door, avoiding the piles of dog feces. Almost as if on cue, the dogs went bonkers again. On the way out the door, Li looked back at Ramsey and shouted. "Hey Terry, why don't you clean up the dog shit?"

"What a piece of work," Li muttered as they walked back to the car.

Drew nodded. "Yeah, I guess in their world, even if your criminal associate gets you tossed in prison and bangs your wife while you're doing the time, as long as the money is good, business is business."

Chapter Thirty

THE FEDERAL TRIAL FOR Tony Dunn and his co-defendants lasted a week. Two days after the jury began deliberations, they returned guilty verdicts for Dunn's three co-defendants. But the jury foreman reported they could not reach a unanimous verdict for Dunn. The judge sent them back twice to resume deliberations, but one of the twelve stubbornly refused to vote guilty with the other eleven. In a criminal offense trial, all twelve jurors had to agree on the judgment. Whether a verdict of guilt or innocence, they had to reach a unanimous decision. Satisfied further deliberations seemed unlikely to produce a unanimous verdict, the presiding judge accepted the trial for Tony Dunn had ended with a deadlocked jury and declared a mistrial.

Later, Drew read in the paper that the US Attorney's Office for the Central District of California had issued a press release stating they had no plans to retry the case against Anthony Dunn unless new compelling evidence surfaced. It wasn't an acquittal, but for the time being, Tony Dunn was off the hook.

To Drew, it seemed Dunn lived a charmed life. Whenever fingers of guilt pointed his way, he somehow always wriggled off the hook. But recalling how ATF Agent Kemp's testimony at the trial had turned lackluster when he spoke about Tony Dunn, but had been compelling when he had spoken about the other defendants, Drew had to wonder if other forces besides luck had been at work. It also seemed curious that while eleven members of Dunn's jury of peers had voted to find him guilty along with the three others, one had obstinately voted innocent again and again. Had someone bribed the lone juror to cause the mistrial? As he had shown before, Dunn wasn't averse to buying himself out of legal trouble.

Still, Dunn's legal problems were far from over. Two weeks after he walked out of federal court in Los Angeles on the mistrial on the arson-for-hire and racketeering charges, the LAPD narcotics cops served a third no-knock search warrant at the Dunn residence and had made another big score. Drew, Estrada, and Li had joined them. Dunn was tired of seeing the three LAPD murder cops as unwanted "guests" in his home. The cops thoroughly searched and pretty much trashed the house again and carted off another load of Dunn's dope, cash, and firearms. This time, Dunn had not commented. By now, the warrant service operations must have seemed routine stuff. But soon, the time would come for him to walk into the Los Angeles Superior Court to answer on a raft of drug charges.

While Drew and his team were aware of Dunn's impending trial, they focused on a trial of their own with bigger stakes. It was June, eleven months after the Wonderland murders had occurred and the trial of John C. Watson got underway.

In his opening statement, Deputy District Attorney Alex Douglas told the seven-woman and five-man jury that he would prove that Watson took part in the murders of four persons and the attempted murder of a fifth victim who sustained grievous injuries that would leave her permanently disabled at the Wonderland house on the past first of July. He described Watson as a perpetual liar with no credibility and that Watson had admitted to letting killers into the home very early in the morning to murder the sleeping victims, knowing full well their intentions.

There could have been no more dramatic way to open a mass-murder trial than by showing the jury the videotape recording made at the crime scene, raw and unedited. Drew took the stand to testify to all he had observed at the crime scene while making his narrated walk-through. It put the case in proper perspective for the jurors right out of the gate. There were more than a few gasps from both jurors and others in the courtroom as the videotape rolled.

Drew also testified that after they released Watson following an interview, during which he had told detectives he would not name the other killers because he feared Tony Dunn, Watson was back at Dunn's residence in Studio City within an hour. Drew stated detectives had also documented several subsequent visits by Watson to the residence over many months, presumably to score drugs.

Finally, Drew testified the LAPD released Watson from the so-called protective custody at the Biltmore Hotel because he lied about anything substantive to the investigation. In a favorable ruling for the prosecution, Judge Barbara Daniels found Watson could not claim coercion as a defense for murder.

The prosecutor called Dennis Mack to the stand next. Mack was sober and sharp for an old ex-con. He described the robbery at Tony Dunn's house he had taken part in, articulating his words almost like an English scholar, leaving nothing out. Mack's testimony was crucial because it laid out the motive for the murders. While establishing motive was not legally required to prove any crime, including murder, it was something juries always seemed to want to know.

Next up came Bob Farmer. Farmer related the same facts that Mack had laid out, but stumbled his way through his testimony. He did, however, corroborate all the important points Mack had testified to.

Oscar Estrada took the stand and testified about Watson's statements during interviews he had taken part in. He testified Watson had admitted to being at the Wonderland house when the murders occurred and to letting the other unknown killers in using a key to the front door murder victim Nancy Poole had given him prior to the murders. Estrada also testified Watson had admitted he knew what would happen at the time he gave the other killers access to the house.

Amy Li testified next to many of the same points as Estrada, corroborating Estrada's testimony. She also testified that on the flight back to Los Angeles after she and Detective Drew had arrested Watson in Florida, Watson had made unsolicited statements to her after detectives had advised him of his Miranda rights previously, that Dunn had forced him to admit to helping set up the robbery at Dunn's residence. Watson had also stated that at the time that had occurred, Dunn had copied the names and addresses of Watson's family members from his phone and threatened to use the information to get even if Watson ever crossed him.

Adrian Preston, one of Watson's defense attorneys, cross-examined Li. Preston was interested in the parts of Li's testimony involving Watson's extreme fear of Tony Dunn, especially the details about Dunn copying the names and addresses of Watson's relatives from his cell phone.

Los Angeles attorneys Clay Dixon and Adrian Preston represented John Watson at the trial. The legal community considered both counselors two of the best and most competent criminal trial lawyers in Los Angeles County. Getting these two excellent attorneys at the county's expense to represent him was probably the best thing that had happened to John Watson since the horrendous events that had taken place at the Wonderland house the previous summer.

Following Li to the stand was pathologist Dr. Nina Garraway from the coroner's office, who had testified previously in hundreds of homicide cases as a medical expert. She described in detail all the horrific wounds the four deceased victims had sustained that were instrumental in causing their deaths. Dr. Garraway also testified to the facts concerning her examination of Dawn Allen, the sole surviving victim, and to the unquestioned similarities of Allen's wounds compared to those of the other four victims.

After the pathologist's testimony, Deputy District Attorney Alex Douglas called a series of experts from the Scientific Investigation Division to the stand to testify regarding forensic evidence collected at the crime scene. One of those, a latent print expert, testified to lifting a bloody partial left-hand print from an ornate bed railing above the battered body of victim Joe Allen and that a print examiner had subsequently identified the print as that of John Watson. She also testified the curious location she had lifted the print from was consistent with a person bracing themselves with the left hand while striking down at the victim's head with a blunt instrument held in the right hand.

The prosecution called Dawn Allen as the people's last witness. She appeared fragile and innocent, almost childlike, as she limped to the witness stand. She wore a hairpiece to conceal her severely damaged skull. Dawn's testimony included her recollections of what had occurred at the Wonderland house after the Dunn robbery, including a drug-fueled party. When the prosecutor asked what she recalled about the attack on her, a palpable hush fell over the courtroom. Dawn stated that all she could remember were shadowy figures in the darkened bedroom holding metallic objects and then tremendous pain that was worse than any pain she had ever felt previously.

In a very delicate cross-examination of Dawn Allen given her obvious medical condition, Clay Dixon settled for getting her to admit that at no time had she observed John Watson in the company of those who had attacked her. Dixon's cross had been brief, to the point, and, in Drew's estimation, very effective.

In the middle of the trial, during a lull in the testimony, a lone male entered the courtroom and sat down in the back row. It was something that happened regularly in high-profile Los Angeles County cases. But usually, such visitors were not also suspects in a murder case being tried. The lone male was Anthony "Tony" Dunn, and in mere seconds, almost everyone in the courtroom recognized him. After only a few minutes, Dunn got up and walked out.

Watson's attorneys called no witnesses, certainly not Watson himself. The defense rested immediately after the prosecution had rested. It was time for the closing arguments.

Chapter Thirty-One

IN HIS CLOSING STATEMENT, Alex Douglas touched on all the salient points of testimony from the many witnesses who had testified in the people's case—the Watson admissions, the bloody palm print and its unique position, and Dennis Mack's testimony about the ill-natured relationship between Watson and Joe Allen. Mack had testified that Joe Allen had often humiliated John Watson by slapping him around when had showed up at the Wonderland house looking to score drugs. He ended his remarks with two questions. "If John Watson did not take part in the murders, why did the other killers allow him to live? Is John Watson sitting here alive today because he delivered the vicious, fatal blows to Joe Allen and is just as guilty of murder as the others?"

Defense counsel Clay Dixon gave the closing statement for the defense. In his remarks, Dixon stated that the prosecution had put the wrong man on trial for the Laurel Canyon murders. This had been the central theme of the defense throughout the trial. The defense attorney said the actual killers had forced Watson at gunpoint to allow them to enter the house and that Watson had complied only because he had genuinely feared for his life and the lives of his relatives. Dixon added that Tony Dunn was an incredibly evil man and that the state should have prosecuted him, not John Watson. Dixon then blasted Alex Douglas and the police.

"The district attorney's office and the LAPD investigators have put John Holmes on trial for one reason," Dixon stated. "Because he wouldn't give up Dunn, the man who ordered the horrific murders. I know what the law states. Coercion is no defense against a charge of murder. But ladies and gentlemen, sitting on a jury does not mean leaving your common sense at home. Ask yourselves this question. What rational person would risk harm to his family and himself by giving evidence against an evil man who had already threatened them with death?"

With the closing arguments completed, Judge Daniels charged the jury, informing them of the applicable law and of what they must do to reach a verdict, and sent them to the jury room to deliberate the fate of John Watson. Deputy DA Alex Douglas and Drew and his team felt confident the jury would find John Watson guilty. But it was not to be.

The jury deliberated less than two full days before returning a not guilty verdict. They acquitted John Watson on all charges. The short time the jury had taken to reach the verdict showed there could not have been much disagreement among the jurors. They had believed the defense's argument that the state should have tried Tony Dunn for the murders, not John Watson.

Once the verdict was in, a disappointed Alex Douglas skipped the press briefing and retired to his office without comment. Drew and his team drove to the Smog Cutter, an East Hollywood dive bar, to lick their wounds and discuss how to move forward with the case after the stinging defeat.

"I can't believe the jury bought the defense's wrong guy on trial argument," Estrada seethed. "They ignored the evidence and just looked for a reason to acquit. It was just like the Simpson trial."

"What now, Howie?" Li asked, sipping her vodka, lime, and soda.

Drew stared at his untouched bottle of Fat Tire Belgian ale. He replied without looking up.

"We regroup and press forward on Tony Dunn," Drew said. "I'm disappointed in the verdict, but we all know Dunn was behind the murders. We have to find the evidence that proves he orders the killings. We get Dunn and we still get some justice for the victims."

"The problem with the case from the start was the victims," Estrada said. "The jury couldn't sympathize with a bunch of druggies and armed robbers. They probably felt like the Wonderland crew brought it on themselves and were no better than the killers."

"Yeah, maybe," Drew said. "But for us, they were murder victims, unjustly deprived of their lives, just like any other murder victim. They deserve justice like everybody else."

Estrada drank some beer and sighed. "You're right Howie, but because of the character of our victims, all we had were other robbers and drug addicts as witnesses, individuals no ordinary citizen understands, much less give credibility to. I have to wonder if trying Dunn would end any differently."

"Our job is investigating murders," Drew said. "We find the evidence that identifies the killers and arrest them. After that, it's out of our hands. We can't worry about what might happen when the lawyers take over. We still have to do our jobs."

With nothing to celebrate, the meeting broke up early. The trial had ended on Friday afternoon and Drew told Li and Estrada to take the weekend off and to be ready to hit it again hard on Monday. They couldn't worry about the one who got away. The team had to focus on Tony Dunn.

Drew, Li, and Estrada hadn't been the only ones holding a meeting. While the cops were mourning John Watson's acquittal, Tony Dunn and Justin Carr were having a conversation inside Dunn's home.

"That homicide detective is my problem," Dunn growled. "As soon as he took over the Wonderland thing, the raids started. He is destroying my business, and he has to go."

"You want to kill a cop, Tony?" Carr said. "I hate that fucker as much as you do. But killing a cop is only going to bring more heat down on us."

"I've got plenty of cops on my payroll," Dunn said. "They need a reminder. It's time to send a message about what happens to people who fuck with Tony Dunn. Get those two Haitians you found for the Wonderland job to go with you. I want that fucking Drew dead before Monday."

"Okay, boss," Carr relented. "I'll make the call and set it up."

"Damn right," Dunn said. He pushed a scrap of paper across the table to Carr. "That's his address. I got it from one of my LAPD contacts. Now get it done, Justin."

Chapter Thirty-Two

MOSTLY TO ASSUAGE HIS guilty feelings, Drew had called Nina Garraway on Friday evening and had invited her to spend the weekend at his place. Drew developed a singular focus when investigating a murder case. As a result, he and Garraway had spent little time together once he got the Wonderland case. He knew the relationship had suffered as a result and wanted to rehabilitate it.

Nina Garraway, a consummate professional herself, understood how driven and obsessed Howard Drew became when he had a case. He was like a dog with a bone and shoved everything else aside to focus on what was most important to him, solving murders and bringing killers to justice. She understood it, but that didn't mean she liked it. But she agreed to accept Howard's invitation.

Howard and Nina spent all day Saturday together and then headed to Long Beach for an early dinner and then the Cowboy Country Saloon to take in a Mustangs of the West concert performance.

Howard had followed the band since 2018, and agreed with the opinion of Bill Bentley that their hit single that year, "T-shirt From California," was "as classic a heart-tugging Southern California song as anything heard since the Eagles were trying to check out of the Hotel California." They had turned many more great songs since then.

Drew especially loved that the talented Aubrey Richmond had joined the band on the fiddle and vocals. Richmond had first hit Howard's country and western music radar when she had appeared on an album produced by Calico the band, another Los Angeles Southern California country band whose music he enjoyed immensely. Country and western music was Howard's thing, not something Nina Garraway had strong feelings about either way. But she didn't mind indulging the one interest she felt he loved outside his job as a homicide detective.

After the concert, the couple got back late to Howard's new home on Passmore Drive in the Hollywood Hills West neighborhood. Drew unlocked the gate, held it open, and then followed Nina down the half dozen stone and masonry steps to the side patio and they went inside.

Drew had built the house, using the inheritance he had received from his paternal grandfather, on a narrow ridge line lot overlooking Nichols Canyon and with a spectacular view of the downtown LA skyline in the distance.

They went to bed and made love for the first time in weeks, but it felt bittersweet for them both. Howard and Nina sensed their relationship was slipping away, and neither really knew what to do about it.

Drew got little sleep with too much on his mind and was up before the sun. He was outside on the back deck smoking a cigarette and on his second cup of black coffee when Nina came out. She had woke and found Howard missing from the bed and then tried to return to sleep, but it hadn't taken her. She leaned against the railing beside Howard, looking at the sunrise.

"You promised you were quitting this time," Nina said, frowning as Howard expelled the smoke from his lungs. "You started again when you got the case."

"Yeah, I know," Drew said. "It was the stress and long hours, I guess. But I'm quitting again."

"Sure, Howie. I've stopped counting how many times I've heard that from you."

"Fine," Drew said. He picked up the cigarette package from the railing and tossed it over the railing into the air. "There. Problem solved."

"Howie! I can't believe you just did that."

"You said you wanted me to quit."

"I want you to quit. But I didn't want you to litter. And I want you to quit for you, not for me. Smoking is a self-destructive habit, and it's just another reason for me to worry about you."

Drew set his coffee cup on the railing, put his arms around her, and pulled her close. He kissed her forehead. "You shouldn't spend your time worrying about me. I'm good. Seriously."

"If you say so," Nina said, pulling away. "I'm going to shower and head home."

"Why?" Drew asked. "I thought you were staying all weekend?"

"I can't, Howie," Nina said, pulling the robe she kept at his place tighter against the chill. "I've got things to do before work tomorrow morning and I've got an early post time for the first of three autopsies."

"Okay," Drew said, looking out at the smog shrouded downtown skyline.

Nina turned and went back inside.

Drew picked up the coffee cup and sipped the now tepid coffee. "Shit," he muttered. "What's going on?" He stayed out on the deck, inhaling the earthy smell of eucalyptus rising from the tall trees in the canyon down below. When he went back inside for his third cup of coffee, Nina had dressed. She kissed him on the cheek, said goodbye, and left out the front door. Suddenly, Drew regretted throwing his only pack of smokes off the deck. He had a feeling Nina wouldn't be coming back.

Drew spent the rest of Sunday reviewing the murder books, focusing on the interviews and who they had talked to but needed to circle back to. He didn't intend to bother with John Watson again anytime soon. The acquittal had removed any leverage they had with him. But somewhere among the names he had listed on the legal pad in front of him was someone who could testify to Tony Dunn's involvement in the murders. He just had to find a way to get them to talk.

In the mid-afternoon, Drew went out for cigarettes and picked up a sandwich. He returned home, ate the sandwich, and then continued his review while listening to the CD he had bought at the concert the night before until two Monday morning. Drew knew he needed to get a few hours of sleep before getting dressed and heading downtown for work. He went into the bathroom and brushed his teeth, seeing the deep lines under his eyes in the mirror. So much for a restful weekend, he thought, turning off the light and padding barefooted down the hall to the bedroom. He opened the window facing the postage stamp front yard, which was below the street above, to get some fresh air. Then he climbed into bed beneath the sheet and comforter, willing himself to sleep.

Chapter Thirty-Three

DREW TOSSED AND TURNED. He glanced at his alarm clock and saw it was almost three. Then, outside the open window, he heard a car door shut. A few moments later, he heard what sounded like someone rattling his steel gate at the top of the steps. Getting out of bed, Drew hurriedly put on a T-shirt and pants. He pulled open the drawer of the nightstand beside the bed and took out his holstered duty weapon and a Pelican flashlight. Drew opened the bedroom door and walked up the hallway to where it opened into the living room. He heard shuffling footsteps on the side patio and then the illumination from a vapor light above the street, backlit someone standing on the patio in front of the glass front door, casting a long shadow on the living room floor.

Drew hastily retreated to the bedroom, tucking the compact Glock into his waistband. He closed the door and then went to the closet and slid back the door. Using the Pelican flashlight, he punched in the combination to the gun safe inside the closet. He removed a blue Kevlar vest and put it on, tightening the Velcro straps. Then he took out a loaded Remington 870 tactical shotgun. After closing the door to the safe and the closet door, Drew went to the open window. He unfastened the screen and let it fall to the ground below the window. Then he climbed out and backed into a dark area in the trees and thick shrubbery growing against the slope of the ridge line and took a knee with the butt of the shotgun pressed into his right shoulder and the muzzle aimed at the window. He flipped off the safety.

Someone, who couldn't have missed his city ride parked in front of the gate, was creeping his house at three in the morning when they knew he was probably at home. That didn't bode well. He had left his phone on the kitchen bar and was on his own.

Justin Carr and the two Haitians, Ricardo Benard and Stanley Georges, the men Dunn had paid to help with the Wonderland job, got out of the Honda Civic Carr had stolen from an apartment complex parking lot two hours before. They crept to the steel gate, each gripping a Taurus TH10 semi-automatic pistol. Benard and Georges were both former Haitian police officers who had gone over to the Port-Au-Prince criminal gangs before traveling to Mexico and illegally crossing the southern border into the United States. Both were violent criminals in South LA.

The three men found the gate locked. Benard climbed over it, dropped, and unlocked it from the interior side. Carr looked at his wristwatch and saw it was almost three. The cop should be fast asleep.

He and Georges passed through the open gate, and Carr closed it behind him quietly. Then they followed Benard down the stone steps to the side patio. "Stay outside and watch in case he wakes up and gets out of the house," Carr whispered to Bernard. After the man nodded his understanding, Carr and Georges advanced to the front glass door. Georges knelt, placing his pistol on the deck and pulled a short pry tool from his hip pocket. He pressed the business end into the gap between the door frame and the jamb and applied pressure. The wooden jamb gave way and the deadbolt and door latch bolt pulled free of the striker plates. Georges stood and pushed the door open, and Carr followed him inside.

The men expected the cop would have a weapon nearby and moved through the house cautiously. The kitchen and living room were empty, and they proceeded down the hall, seeing a closed door at the end. They glanced inside the open door of a bedroom and bathroom as they made their way toward the closed door. Georges turned the knob and opened the door slowly. In the dim light, they saw the bed was empty, with the bed coverings turned back as though someone had been in the bed. Dunn checked the en suite bathroom and found it empty. Georges had moved to a window and found it open with no screen in place. First, he turned and told Carr that the cop much have heard them and got outside. Then he pushed the curtains aside and leaned out.

"Ricardo, he's outside," he said sharply in French, but without shouting.

Drew saw the man plainly when he stepped in front of the bedroom window and leaned out. He also saw the handgun in the man's right hand.

He put the beaded sight of the Remington on the man's center mass. Just as the man said something, probably to someone outside the house, Drew fired, rapidly worked the pump action, and fired again. The man in the window disappeared. Drew swung the muzzle to his right, catching movement. Another man armed with a pistol had turned the corner of the house, but started backing up when Drew had cut loose with the shotgun. But he didn't move fast enough and Drew unloaded two more blasts of 12-gauge 00 buckshot. He saw the man go down on his back.

When the twin shotgun blasts blew Georges away from the window, Carr had first dived to the floor. But he scrambled up quickly and raced down the hallway to the door they had entered. He had heard two more shotgun blasts before he reached the door. Instead of taking the side patio back to the steps, he sprinted around a corner to a back deck and ran to the far end, vaulted a side railing, and landed on his hands and knees in a narrow side yard. He got up, ran to the privacy fence, and scrambled over it.

Drew dropped the empty shotgun and pulled the Glock from his waistband. He strode to the man on the ground at the corner of the house. He saw the subject was unmoving and could make out the wetness on the front of his shirt. Drew kicked the semi-automatic pistol away and then moved in a crouch around the corner just in time to see someone disappear around the far corner of the side patio and onto the rear deck. He figured the subject would jump the fence into the neighbor's backyard. Instead of pursuing him, Drew sprinted up the steps to his gate. He opened it, did a quick peek toward the neighbor's house, and then sprinted in that direction. When he reached the neighbor's brick mailbox enclosure, Drew assumed a barricaded position with his arms extended over the top of the mailbox with the muzzle aimed at the wooden privacy fence gate at the top of the brick-lined stair steps.

The gate flew open and a man holding a handgun emerged. Even in the low light conditions, Drew recognized the man instantly.

"LAPD!" Drew shouted. "Put down the weapon, Carr!"

Justin Carr skidded to a stop halfway down the steps toward Drew. But instead of dropping the pistol, he raised his hands slightly above his shoulders as if surrendering, but still gripping the pistol in his right hand. Drew recognized the look of indecision on Carr's face as he assessed his situation.

"Don't do it!" Drew shouted. But Carr dropped his hands and Drew fired twice in rapid succession, the bullets striking Carr in the chest. He dropped the pistol and fell backwards onto the steps, and then slid down two more steps before coming to rest. Drew climbed the steps, kicked the pistol away, and pressed two fingertips to Carr's neck. He found no pulse.

Drew turned, jogged back to his gate and into the house. He first checked his bedroom and found the third man dead on the floor beside the window. Then he raced back to the kitchen, grabbed his phone, and stepped back out onto the side patio. He dialed nine-one-one.

When the emergency operator answered, Drew identified himself as a police officer and gave his badge number. "Shots fired, 5209 Passmore Drive. I have three suspects down with gunshot wounds. Send an RA unit and a supervisor."

After hanging up, Drew called Lieutenant Moreno. A groggy sounding Moreno answered after five rings. Drew filled him in briefly on what had just happened at his home.

"Jesus, Howie! Three dead?"

"They gave me no choice, Lieutenant. I have an RA unit and patrol on the way, but you might want to respond. Also, I need you to call Li and tell her I want her to meet me at FID to rep for me."

A Force Investigation Division investigator took possession of Drew's shotgun and Glock and then transported him downtown to the FID offices at the Professional Standards Bureau on North Figueroa Street. Li was waiting for them in the lobby when they arrived and went upstairs to a FID office for the interview. Once everyone sat down with and Drew across a table, the FID investigator switched on a recorder and began the interview. He read Drew his rights and reminded him of his duty under California law and department policy to cooperate with the investigation.

"Briefly explain the incident and how it transpired in your own words, Detective."

Drew explained he had gone to bed but could not fall asleep. Then he had heard suspicious noises and had gone to investigate. After discovering unknown subjects appeared to be making entry into his house, he had secured his personal home defense weapon and his duty weapon before climbing out his bedroom window as the suspects forced entry.

"Then what happened?"

"I found a place of concealment in my backyard and saw an armed subject inside my bedroom at the window, and fired at him twice with my Remington 870."

"Did you identify yourself before firing?"

"There were three armed assailants intending to kill him," Li said. "That would not have been tactically sound or reasonable under the circumstances."

The investigator glared at Li. "Detective Li, you are here as an advocate, not a participant in this interview." He turned his attention back to Drew.

Li crossed her arms and sighed.

"No, I did not. I was outnumbered and outgunned."

"Did you try to deescalate by removing yourself from the situation?"

"Not feasible. I didn't know where all the individuals were at the time. They were armed, and I didn't feel I could safely exit the area on foot."

"Okay, you fired on the subject at the window inside your home, then what?"

"I sensed movement and saw a second armed subject come around the corner of the house and engaged him with the shotgun."

"Did you announce yourself and give a warning that time?"

"I did not. It happened fast. I saw the raised weapon, and under threat of death or serious bodily injury, I fired twice center mass, striking the individual."

"When did you call for backup?"

"I didn't call for backup. I had left my phone on the kitchen bar before going to bed and did not have access to it. Because I was off duty, I didn't have access to a police radio."

"All right, after you shot the second subject, what happened?"

"I moved to the side patio and saw a third individual round the corner onto the back deck. Believing he was going to climb the privacy fence between my side yard and neighbor's property, I moved to the street and towards the front of my neighbor's home."

"Anticipating that you would intercept the third subject?"

"That's correct."

"Then what happened?"

"He came through the neighbor's gate and descended the steps toward me. I was in a barricaded position, and believing he was the last of the group, I announced myself as an LAPD police officer and verbally commanded him to put down his weapon."

"Did he comply?"

"No, instead of putting the weapon down, he raised his hands slightly above his shoulders as if surrendering, but he kept the weapon in his right hand as he did so."

"And then?"

"I assume he believed he could shoot me before I shot him. He dropped both arms, pointing the weapon, and I fired twice, striking him in the chest area. He dropped the weapon and fell to the steps."

"Did you render aid to any of the subjects?"

"Yes, I checked all three for signs of life. I ran back to the house and got my phone, called nine-one-one and requested an RA unit."

"Were all three deceased at that time?"

"Yes."

The investigator nodded and switched off the recorder. "That's enough for now, Detective. I'll call you if we have additional questions as we proceed with the use of force investigation."

"Great," Drew said. He and Li got up and left the office. In the lobby, they met Lieutenant Moreno.

"You okay, Howie?" Moreno asked, with apparent genuine concern.

"Yes, Lieutenant. I'm good."

"Okay, well, you've had a long night. No one has told me to suspend you administratively pending the completion of the use of force investigation. Seems cut and dried to me, so I don't think that will happen. But take the day off to rest up. You can report to work tomorrow morning unless something changes before then."

"That's unnecessary, Lieutenant. Li can give me a ride back to my place. I'll shower and change and after I get someone on the way to secure my house, I'll be in for work."

"Well, if you're sure," Moreno said. "But just come in when you can. Take all the time you need to square things away at home."

"Okay, thanks, Lieutenant."

They left the building together and Li drove Drew home.

Chapter Thirty-Four

DREW GOT TO THE OFFICE at the PAB shortly after nine on Monday morning. He had found a contractor to repair the front door, his bedroom window, and the damaged drywall in the bedroom perforated by shotgun pellets when he had fired at the subject in front of the window. Luckily, the suspect had absorbed most of them. He had also hired a commercial crime scene cleaning company to remove the biological remains in the bedroom after the SID criminalists had finished their work inside his home. Drew had worked many crime scenes, but never had expected to live inside one.

Estrada and Li were both at their desks when he walked in.

"I just heard about your busy night, brother," Estrada said. "You okay, Howie?"

"Yeah, I'm good," Drew said, shrugging out of his sports coat, ready to get down to work.

"You think they were the same guys that did the Wonderland murders?" Estrada asked.

"Well, we all believed Carr was one of the actual killers and he's off the board now. I don't know who the other two were yet."

"Hopefully, you bagged them all," Li said. "I'm just sorry you almost got killed doing it."

"Well, we took a swing at Watson and missed," Drew said. "If it turns out Carr and the other two dead guys were the actual Wonderland killers, then all we have to do is tie Dunn to it."

"Yes, the hard part is over and we just have to clean it up by nailing Dunn," Li chuckled. "I wish it were that easy."

"We'll get there," Drew said. "We just have to keep working it. Someone out there knows what we need to put Dunn away. We have probably already talked to them. Now we have to identity who that person is and get them to talk."

"Who we starting with?" Estrada asked.

Before Drew could reply, Moreno walked into their area and told them he wanted to talk to them in his office. Li, Drew, and Estrada got up and followed their boss to the glass box. Moreno told them to grab a seat and sat down behind his desk.

"First, you guys have nothing to hang your heads about after Watson's acquittal," Moreno said. "You all did some good police work, and you found enough evidence to get a conviction. Juries are screwy and unpredictable. But it's the system we've got and what we must work with."

Drew wondered what was up with the pep talk. They were all veteran cops, and no one was hanging their head over something they couldn't control. Then the other shoe dropped.

"Murders are up and we're still short handed. I have to pull Oscar off the Wonderland case and put him back with his old partner. And I'm putting you all back in the rotation."

Moreno's decision left Drew dumbfounded, especially after what happened at his home overnight. "Let me get this straight, Lieutenant. Just because Watson got acquitted, we're going to deep six a case where five people got their heads beat in and move on with our lives? We still have Tony Dunn to consider. And I think we all know who was behind the hit at my place this morning."

"No, Howie, it isn't like that. I want you and Amy to devote as much time to the Wonderland case as you can. But when your number comes up, you will have to take other cases. That's all. I'm pulling Oscar because you have had nothing new in a long while and I can't justify tying up three investigators on a case that is dead in the water for now."

Drew knew there was no point in arguing. It seemed clear Moreno had decided the issue, probably with the backing of Captain Meyers, assuming he hadn't simply dictated the changes to Moreno himself.

"Fine," Moreno said. "Oscar, you're back with Fisher, effective immediately." Moreno stood, picked up a file from his desk, and handed it to Drew. "I'm assigning this one to you and Amy."

Drew flipped open the file and read the name at the top: Colin Knight. He scanned the summary. Hollywood patrol officers responding to a shots fired call in the sixty-nine-hundred block of Woodrow Wilson Drive had discovered Knight, a fifty-two-year-old character actor, shot to death in the driveway beneath the carport of his Hollywood Hills home. The West Bureau detectives had found no evidence of robbery or forced entry into his residence.

"Get started on that one and put whatever spare time you have into the Wonderland murders," Moreno said. "Let's get to work."

"Fucking actors," Li said as the detectives left Moreno's office. "They act like any Hollywood type vic who had a part in a movie is a celebrity and they dump the case on Homicide Special. I've never even heard of this guy."

"Well, it's too bad you guys will no longer benefit from my expert backgrounding skills then," Estrada said sarcastically.

Drew thought he might have heard the name but knew nothing about Knight's acting career. All he knew was just a few days after the first anniversary of the Wonderland murders, he and Li were starting over with a new murder investigation.

Estrada boxed up the stuff from the temporary workstation he had used while working with Drew and Li.

"Well, guess I'll see you guys around," he said. "I better get over and see what Tom has going and have him bring me up to speed."

Drew sensed Oscar wasn't happy with the changes. Neither was he. He had been skeptical when Moreno had added him to the team, but after working with Estrada, Drew had come to trust the man and respected his skills as an investigator.

"Maybe something will break loose and we will get the band back together," Drew said. "You're a solid murder cop, Oscar, and I hate having our team broken up."

"What are you going to do, right?" Estrada said with a crooked grin. "I enjoyed working with you guys and just wish we could have seen the case through to the end. Good luck with it." With that, Estrada turned with the cardboard box in his hands and ambled across the squad to link up with his former partner, Tom Fisher.

Li thumbed through the file on Colin Knight, their new victim. "What do you want to do first, Howie?"

"I want to see the crime scene," Drew said. "And it is close to my house, so I want to swing by to check on how the contractor is doing on the repairs."

"Did you have breakfast?" Li asked.

"No, didn't have time."

"Neither did I. I woke up late. Since we don't have a body waiting for us at the crime scene, let's stop and get breakfast at the Nickel before we leave downtown."

"You're on, partner," Drew said.

Chapter Thirty-Five

THREE WEEKS AFTER GETTING the Knight murder case, Drew and Li were back at the CCB for court. The detectives hadn't turned up anything new on the Wonderland murders, but Tony Dunn's legal problems were heating up. Deputy DA Alex Douglas had merged the three search warrants, and the evidence collected from them into one case he would prosecute in one trial. Since Drew and Li had attended all three warrant services, Douglas had called them to testify.

Drew and Li had visited briefly with Douglas in his office on the twelfth floor before taking the stairs down to the ninth floor courtroom. Douglas had told them besides the trial on the narcotics distribution and possession charges, he had impaneled a grand jury seeking to indict Dunn for the Wonderland murders. Douglas had subpoenaed John Watson to appear before the grand jury, hoping since Watson had gained an acquittal, and no longer faced legal jeopardy, the man would finally testify against Tony Dunn. But it hadn't worked out. Watson refused to appear before the grand jury. Judge Tabitha Brooks had then jailed Watson for contempt, saying he could sit in jail until he changed his mind about testifying.

Because the defense had invoked the rule to exclude witnesses from the courtroom so they couldn't hear the testimony of other witnesses, Drew and Li were sitting on a bench outside the courtroom at the end of a deserted corridor when a break in the trial occurred. Dunn and his attorneys exited the courtroom. Drew and Li noticed Dunn seemed highly agitated, understandable under the circumstances. He saw Drew and Li sitting down the corridor and after brushing off obvious pleases from his lawyers, Dunn strode toward them.

"You two aren't narcotics cops, you are homicide detectives," Dunn sputtered. "Why are you bothering with me? Why do you care? I want to know."

"Because we've made you our special project," Drew said. "Does that answer your questions, Tony?"

"How do we make this go away?" Dunn asked. "What do you want? How much? Just tell me. A million? A million and a half?"

"Fuck off, Tony," Drew said, getting to his feet. "We aren't for sale. You ordered the Wonderland murders, and you sent Carr after me. We're not stopping until you're in prison for life where you belong."

Dunn turned away and stormed off in a huff. Having picked up on at least some of the conversation, the two lawyers grimaced. Having their client trying to bribe two LAPD detectives in their presence had not pleased them.

The detectives had still not testified when the lunch break rolled around. They walked down to Grand Central Market on South Broadway to lunch at Tacos y Tumbras a Tomas. There were tortas and burritos on the menu, and tacos there were more than satisfying for a quick lunch. The restaurant's meats selections, carne asada, carnitas, and birria, regardless of choice, got piled liberally onto the requisite corn tortillas. Considering the portion sizes, the menu was better priced than other selections at the market.

"You think we should talk to Douglas about Dunn's offer this morning?" Li said between bites. "It's another felony he could stack on him."

"We know how Dunn operates in his nasty little world of drugs, depravity, and destruction," Drew said. "You think he's really willing to the roll the dice with us considering all the publicity surrounding his court case? Maybe his plan was to turn the tables on us."

"How would he expect to pull it off?" Li asked.

"He would probably expect us to circle back to him wearing a wire to accept his offer," Drew said.

"Then we would get him on tape offering us a bribe."

"That would be all well and good," Drew said. "Until he flipped the script on us by denying he offered us a bribe and claimed we solicited him. Since it would be on tape and discoverable, his lawyers would have a field day dirtying us up as corrupt cops. Then they would own us if the DA ever charged him on the Wonderland murders when it got to trial."

"Maybe you're right, Howie."

"There's even a worse case scenario I can think of."

"Worst case?"

"Yeah, Dunn wearing a wire when we came back to him pretending to discuss accepting a payoff. Under that scenario, Dunn could easily make it appear that we were trying to shake him down for a bribe. Dunn is that devious and crafty. I think we should just forget it. We have plenty on our plates already, anyway."

At the end of the week, the jury returned a verdict. Unlike the outcome of the People versus John C. Watson, the jury didn't acquit Anthony "Tony" Dunn on the seven counts of possession for the distribution of a controlled substance. They returned a unanimous guilty verdict on all counts. A month later, the presiding Los Angeles County judge sentenced Dunn to eight years in a California state prison. It wasn't the sentence the homicide detectives really wanted, but at least Tony Dunn was off the streets and couldn't hurt anyone else for a while. But the story didn't end with the conviction.

While Tony Dunn was at Bauchet awaiting transfer to state prison, Drew received a call from a jail staff member. Dunn wanted to talk to the detectives about the Wonderland murders. Drew figured it was just another of Dunn's schemes, but didn't feel he could ignore the request. So, he and Li, feeling some trepidation and a lot of skepticism, drove over to Men's Central to talk with Dunn.

A jailer brought Dunn into a visiting attorney's room to speak to the detectives. Once seated, Dunn began complaining he was a businessman and did not understand why the justice system was persecuting him.

Drew ignored his rant and got straight to the point. "What did you wish to discuss, Tony? Why are we here?"

"I know who one killer was," Dunn stated.

"Who?" Drew asked, not concealing his skepticism.

"That biker guy, Dennis Mack."

"And how do you know that, Tony?"

"In my business, people tell me things. And I know it's true."

"You have evidence to back it up? Someone we can talk to who will corroborate your story?"

"Not really," Dunn said. "I just know, that's all."

"Bullshit," Drew said. He and Li stood up.

"We have better things to do than listen to your crap," Li said. "Like putting other criminals like you in jail."

The detectives walked out of the room to a barrage of profanity-laden expletives hurled at their backs by Dunn and continued down the corridor to the exit.

Chapter Thirty-Six

DREW AND LI MADE STEADY progress on their investigation of the murder of actor Colin Knight. While delving into Knight's background, they discovered that the New York-born Knight had an extensive rap sheet. He had burglary, grand theft, and fraud arrests dating back thirty years. The US Secret Service had arrested him a decade before his death for possession of two hundred thousand dollars in counterfeit US currency. Knight had cut a deal with the feds and had testified against another conspirator who got convicted. In return, he got probation and escaped going to federal prison. More recently, police had arrested Knight for cocaine possession, not unusual as far as the Hollywood crowd went.

As an actor, Knight had performed minor roles in several motion pictures but had acted in over a hundred episodes in various popular television crime dramas, always typecast as a villainous mob character. He had evidently been the consummate New York tough guy mobster his entire acting career. Li and Drew thought it ironic that someone had shot him to death in real life in much the same fashion as the characters he had played in movies and television. Maybe he had tried to be a tough guy in real life?

Given his criminal record, Drew and Li had considered three separate motive theories for the murder—one involving drugs, and another involving counterfeit money. But they soon settled on a third theory, the well-worn and familiar love triangle angle, after interviewing one of Knight's longtime friends.

"This was a love triangle deal," Scott Wheeler told the detectives. Wheeler was another actor who told Drew and Li he had known Knight for over a dozen years.

"Some other guy said, 'Stay away from my girlfriend.' Colin didn't listen, and the guy went and hired some knuckleheads to do the deal."

Wheeler told them it seemed ironic that Knight had died because he hadn't heeded his own advice.

"Colin once told me, 'Scott, no matter what you do, never get whacked over a woman. Women are like buses. There'll always be another one.' "

The interview with Wheeler and a neighbor and the evidence suggested the case might very well also have a murder-for-hire angle. The day the detectives visited the crime scene, a neighbor told them he had heard no gunshots, but had seen two figures scuffling with Christi next to the carport sometime earlier on the morning that the police had found him dead. Also, at autopsy, a pathologist had removed two bullets from Knight, but bullets that came from two different handguns, suggesting at least two assailants.

As the detectives continued interviewing others who had known Knight, they found more support for their motive theory. Knight had a reputation as a ladies' man, and a successful one. Few of the people they interviewed had seemed to like Knight and had little positive to say about him. Knight had few friends. Many had described him as overbearing, obnoxious, and an "in-your-face" type of person. Just talking to many of Knight's acquaintances left Drew and Li feeling that he probably, either subconsciously or consciously, try to act out the tough-guy roles he played as an actor in his personal life and had alienated many people.

Unable to find any witnesses who could point them to the principals or a wife or girlfriend Knight had supposedly had an affair with, the Knight case lost momentum. Nothing new had surfaced in the Wonderland killings investigation, either. Eventually, Drew and Li moved on to other cases that Lieutenant Moreno assigned them.

After spending two months in county jail, John Watson had agreed to testify before the grand jury. But when he appeared, Watson told one contradicting story after another about his relationship with Tony Dunn. He again admitted he had set up the Dunn robbery, and when Dunn found out about it, he had forced him to let the killers into the Wonderland house. But Watson swore he had never actually seen the killers. Again, he claimed he left the scene after unlocking the front door and had not been involved in the murders. He denied ever hearing Tony Dunn or anyone else ordering the killings.

John Watson gained his release and moved in with an infatuated pornography magazine scribe who had written several articles claiming the district attorney's office and the police were persecuting John Watson only because of his involvement in the pornography industry. She drew comparisons between Watson's incarceration with the way the Russian government jailed dissidents.

Meanwhile, twenty-one months after Tony Dunn had gone to prison, Drew and Li received more discouraging news from Deputy DA Alex Douglas. Dunn appeared in court with his newest attorney, Emmitt Wallace. Wallace had filed a motion requesting the court to release Dunn from Folsom Prison early because he had a sinus tumor and needed surgery.

The attorney had dug up a quack doctor who testified that, in his professional opinion, the state prison system could not provide Dunn adequate medical care. Livid, Douglas opposed the motion, but Judge Bernard Stephens had seemed unreceptive to the prosecutor's arguments. He reduced Dunn's sentence from the original eight-year maximum to four years, making Dunn eligible immediately for parole.

A month later, the California State Department of Corrections Board of Parole released Dunn from prison before he had even served two years of his newly reduced sentence. Not long afterwards, talk of an investigation into an alleged two hundred fifty thousand dollar payoff to Judge Stephens in return for the Dunn prison sentence reduction surfaced. Allegedly, a former bail bondsman, none other than Terry Ramsey, had paid the bribe on Dunn's behalf. Shortly after the investigation began, Judge Stephens resigned from the bench. One of the first things the investigation into Judge Stephens uncovered was that he had a longstanding addiction to cocaine.

If they thought Dunn's latest gaming of the system to once again escape justice was bad news, Drew and Li were soon to face a much larger problem that would affect them in a far more personal way.

Chapter Thirty-Seven

DREW KNEW THAT FOR most people, Monday was the most disliked day of the work week. He always assumed that was because many people found the transition from a more relaxed weekend routine to the demands and stresses of work obligations difficult. But Drew felt the opposite. He always felt eager for the weekend to end so he could return to work. But when he entered the PAB lobby and found Li lurking near the elevators with a troubled expression on her face, Drew had a premonition this Monday would not be a fun day.

"What's up?" Drew asked as Li intercepted him.

"Howie, I think we've got trouble. Moreno told me he wants to see us in his office the minute you walked in."

"Yeah, what about?"

"I don't know. He didn't tell me anything. But he has come out of his office looking for you every five minutes since he talked to me. And there are a couple of IAD suits in his office with him."

Drew looked at his watch. "We don't even go on the clock for fifteen more minutes."

"What do you think is going on, Howie? Have we pissed someone off? Is there a story we need to get straight before we go in?"

"I take it you have never dealt with IAD," Drew said.

"No. FID twice, but never IA. That's the extent of my experience with Professional Standards."

"I don't know what's going on, Amy. Maybe we caught a citizen complaint. But I can't think of anyone we've talked to lately that had a problem with us. We have done nothing wrong, so it couldn't be a big deal."

"Howie, they don't bring IAD in when something isn't a big deal. Something is on."

"Relax, Amy. Let's go upstairs and see what it's about. I still don't think it's a big deal."

"Give me a minute to get back upstairs before you come up," Li said. "I don't want it to appear obvious I was down here talking to you. They might think we are hiding something."

Drew chuckled. "Okay, if it's stressing you that much. Go on up. I'll wait two minutes and then I'll come up."

"Okay, Howie." Li darted into the elevator when the doors opened after someone else had pressed the call button.

Li was at her desk when Drew walked through the door. When he got to his desk, the first thing he noticed was the Wonderland murder books were gone. He had been looking through them and had left them stacked on the desk Friday evening when he left the office.

Moreno came around the corner, spotted him, and said three words. "Drew! My office." Then he turned back towards his office.

"Let's get it over with," Li said from behind Drew. Together, they walked to Moreno's office. Through the glass, Drew saw the backs of two suits sitting in Moreno's office. He had dealt with IAD before, but not with the two guys sitting in the office. He had never had the displeasure of meeting them. But he knew who they were. Stanley and Livingston. They had the rep for being tier-one pricks.

Someone had brought in two more chairs, which made it a little crowded inside the ten by ten office.

"What's this about?" Drew said, pointing at the missing murder books stacked on Moreno's desk.

"Sit down," Moreno said. "Both of you."

"Well, well, Amy," Drew said, eyeing the two IAD detectives. "Looks like we may be part of a Stanley and Livingston expedition. Meet the star pricks of the Internal Affairs Division."

The faces of both IAD detectives flushed with anger.

"I guess the rumors are true," Stanley said. "You think you're funny, but you're not. Well, my advice is to do yourself a favor by keeping your smart mouth shut, Drew. You're in serious trouble."

"What did I do?" Drew asked. "Mis-gender someone in a report? Use the wrong pronouns. Is that what this is about?"

"Knock it off, Drew," Moreno said. "This is a serious matter, and I expect you to treat it that way. Just shut up for a minute. What this is about..."

"I want a lawyer," Drew interrupted.

"So do I," Li said.

"Jesus Christ!" Moreno exclaimed. "We aren't bringing lawyers or the Protective League into it right now. You want to do that, you do it later. Right now, you're both going to sit here and answer some questions."

For a few moments, no one said anything. Moreno glanced out at the squad room and noticed a group of detectives acting like they were working, but actually trying to see if they could see or hear anything to reveal what was going on in the lieutenant's office. He got up and lowered the blinds, telegraphing to everyone in the squad room it was something big.

Moreno sat back down and stabbed an index finger down on the stack of murder books.

"Okay, let's get to it," he said. "First, you two are off the Wonderland case for now. No discussion. Next, you're both going to cooperate and answer the questions Detectives Stanley and Livingston have. Otherwise, you will both get suspended pending further disciplinary action."

Livingston opened his briefcase and pulled out a micro recorder. He switched it on and put it on Moreno's desk with the microphone pointed towards Drew and Li.

"That's bullshit," Drew said, pointing at the recorder. "You want me to cooperate, turn it off."

Moreno audibly exhaled. "Turn it off," he said to Livingston, pointing at the recorder. The IAD detective picked it up and switched it off before putting it back down on the desk. Moreno eyed Drew and Li.

"You're here because a federal law enforcement officer and two other individuals have made serious accusations of corruption to IAD about your conduct during the Wonderland murders investigation. The accusations also involve Detective Estrada, but he isn't here with you only because he is out on a crime scene. These detectives will interview him later today."

When Moreno had said federal law enforcement and then mentioned accusations, one name immediately leaped to Drew's mind. "You're talking about Kemp at the ATF. Am I right?" he said.

"Listen, Drew," Stanley said. "It's clear you don't understand how this works. You aren't in charge and you don't get to ask questions. That's our job. Your job is answering questions. Got it?"

"Got it," Drew said with sarcasm.

"So, you admit to knowing ATF Agent Kemp?" Livingston asked.

"Yes, I've had the displeasure of meeting him," Drew said. "He came in the office throwing his considerable weight around and demanded we turn over everything we had on Tony Dunn. He said he was part of some task force investigating Dunn's involvement in an arson scheme. We politely declined to share."

"Did Agent Kemp provide you with information concerning Tony Dunn and the Wonderland murders?" Livingston asked.

"You ever dealt with the feds, Livingston?" Drew said. "The feds take. They don't give. Oh, wait. You wouldn't know about that. You ride a desk except when you're out harassing cops who do actual police work."

"Okay, that's enough, Drew," Moreno said. "You're saying Agent Kemp gave you no actionable information concerning the Wonderland case?"

"He didn't give us jack shit, Lieutenant," Drew said. "Kemp demanded information from us about a suspect in an active murder investigation and we explained we couldn't help him. He left in a huff without another word. The only other time I've seen him was in federal court when he testified during the arson trial involving Dunn and we didn't speak."

"I've got a meeting in a few minutes," Moreno said. "So, let me summarize the situation for you, Drew, before I turn this over to Detectives Stanley and Livingston. Three individuals have made credible accusations that they gave important information to you and your team that should have enabled you to identify those responsible for the Wonderland murders and believe your team did not follow up because you are protecting Tony Dunn."

"That's bullshit," Drew said. "We worked our asses off trying to connect Tony Dunn to the murders because we know he ordered them. No one has given us any actionable leads that we haven't followed up on. Christ, Lieutenant, someone is just trying to derail the Wonderland investigation. Don't you see that?"

"Yes, something is going on," Moreno said. "But I don't know what it is, and until Internal Affairs scrutinizes the accusations and finishes their investigation, you and Li are off the case. Estrada is already off it. And that's an order."

Moreno was quiet for a moment before continuing.

"You know, Drew, I didn't have to take you into Homicide Special. I could have said no. But I didn't. I recognized your skills and gave you an opportunity. People told me you were good, but that you don't stay inside the lines. Maybe they were right about you, and I should have given more consideration to those opinions. I just hope you haven't done something that will make me regret giving you a chance."

Moreno stood up and looked at the IAD detectives. "I've got to get to a meeting. You men can have the office as long as you need it." He then walked out and closed the door behind him.

"We've heard all about you, Drew," Stanley said. "Well, I think you are toast this time. And this will be a better department when you're no longer a part of it."

Livingston reached over and switched the recorder back on. He recited the date and time, names of those present in the room, and the Internal Affairs case number assigned to the investigation.

"We will begin with you, Detective Drew," he said. Turning to Li, he added, "Detective Li. Please step outside. We will interview you after we've finished with Detective Drew."

Li shot Drew a look of sympathy and then walked out, closing the door behind her.

"Detective Drew, we would like to ask you questions about the investigation of the murders that occurred on Wonderland Avenue last July first. Please tell us of any current or past association you have or have had with Tony Dunn."

"I refuse to answer questions without an attorney present," Drew said. "I invoke my right to representation under the California Public Safety Officers Procedural Bill of Rights Act."

"Detective Drew, department policy requires you to answer our questions," Stanley said. "If you do not cooperate and answer our questions, you will be subject to suspension and possible..."

Drew slapped his left palm sharply with his right hand. "Hey, get your hands off me and stop hitting me!" he shouted. "You think you're going to beat a confession out of me?"

"No one struck Detective Drew and there are two witnesses in the room who can attest to it," Livingston said angrily into the microphone of the recorder.

"Yeah, the two IA goons who just smacked me!" Drew shouted. "This violates my civil rights. I demand an attorney and a rep before we continue before someone gets hurt."

Livingston switched off the recorder and glared at Drew. "Okay, smart guy," he said. "You know what, Drew? Kicking your ass off the force is going to be a genuine pleasure."

"We will have the suspension papers on the chief's desk before lunch, Drew," Stanley added. "You've skated on several questionable use of force investigations and you beat the rap the last time you attracted IAD attention. But not this time, asshole. You're done."

Drew stood. "Well, then I guess we're done here, Bert and Ernie." He opened the door, stepped out, and slammed it behind him, rattling the glass. Avoiding the open-mouth stares of the other detectives, Drew walked through the squad room back to his desk.

"You stay away from the case, Drew!" Stanley shouted after him from the office doorway. "You got that?"

Drew ignored him and kept walking. He found Li sitting at her desk with a questioning look on her face.

"What did they say?" Li said.

"Who cares?" Drew replied. "I'm off the case and those two pricks are going to put suspension papers in on me before the end of the day. If those two pinheads from IAD can take my badge, they can have it."

"What are we going to do?" Li asked in a panicky tone.

"I don't want to drag you down with me, Amy. You do what you feel is best for you. But they aren't railroading me. I'm not answering any of their questions until I have a lawyer and I'm going over to the Protective League right now to get representation."

"Has it come to that?" Li asked. "We've done nothing wrong. Those accusations are ridiculous."

"I think we would be foolish not to get representation. I've had it out with the IAD before and I know how it works. You're guilty unless you can prove you're innocent. I'll take the suspension or temporary relief from duty. That's all they can do. A recommendation for dismissal has to go before the police commission, and I'm not worried about that."

"Did they say anything about me?" Li asked.

"No, but they will be out here to get you as soon as they smooth the feathers I ruffled in there."

Drew's phone rang. He answered. "Yes, that's right." Drew's expression changed from frustrated to surprised. "Ah, okay. I'll be right over." He hung up.

"Who was that?" Li asked.

"That was the break on the Knight case we've been waiting for," Drew said. "That was a chaplain over at Dignity Hospice in Glendale. They have a terminal cancer patient there who wants to get something off his chest. Says he knows all about the murder of Colin Knight."

Li jumped to her feet and grabbed her jacket off the back of her chair. "Well, let's go."

"Hang on, Amy. You better stay here and talk to the IAD guys or you will be in the same boat I am."

"Fuck that," LI said, heading for the door. "We can call the Protective League on the way to Glendale."

Chapter Thirty-Eight

WHILE LI DROVE THEM to the hospice facility in Glendale, Drew called the Los Angeles Police Protective League (LAPPL), the police union representing LAPD officers up to the rank of lieutenant. The representative he talked to told Drew they would reach out to a union lawyer and someone would call them back. After he disconnected the call, Drew turned off his phone. He already had six missed calls from Lieutenant Moreno and had no intention of calling him back until they talked to the guy at the hospice.

Li pulled into the lot of the one-story brick building, and parked. She and Drew went inside. Drew identified himself to the receptionist and asked to speak with the chaplain. A few minutes after the receptionist made a call, a thin man with gray hair wearing a black suit and a white clerical collar met them in the lobby. After the introductions, the chaplain led them down a corridor and stopped in front of a door.

"The patient's name is Woody Stokes," the chaplain explained. "He has lung cancer, which had already metastasized before he sought treatment and there was nothing the doctors could do. Woody asked me to call you. He seems remorseful and wants to do the right thing before he passes."

"How bad off is he?" Drew asked.

"I'm afraid he doesn't have much time left. Weeks, a month maybe, at best."

"Is he lucid?"

"Oh, yes. He is receiving palliative care for pain relief, but in possession of his faculties."

Drew nodded, and the chaplain opened the door. Li and Drew followed him into the room.

"Woody, the police detectives are here to see you," the chaplain announced.

Even the blanket and sheet covering the man didn't hide the emaciated appearance of his frail body.

"Hi, guys," the man said weakly.

Drew and Li saw the nasal cannula inside his nostrils, the IV tubing extending from the needle in a vein in his left hand that ran to the bags suspended above the bed, and the half-filled catheter bag attached to the hospital bedside.

"Hello, Mr. Stokes," Drew said. "I'm LAPD Detective Drew and this is my partner, Detective Li."

"Call me Woody, Detective," the man said with a chuckle, soon followed by a fit of coughing that left Stokes gasping for breath.

Drew nodded. "I'm sorry you aren't well, Woody," Drew said. "You wanted to talk to us?"

"Are you investigating the murder of that actor, Colin Knight?" Stokes asked.

"That's right."

"Okay, good. Well, it was me and two other guys who killed him at his house on Woodrow Wilson Drive."

"Do you mind if we record your statement, Woodrow?" Drew asked.

"No, go ahead. That's why I asked the chaplain to call. I want it on the record."

Drew nodded at Li. She switched on the recorder she had brought and placed in on the over-bed table.

Drew recited the date, time, and location and then identified himself and Li, including their badge numbers. Then he asked Stokes to give his name and date of birth. After Stokes finished, Drew asked him to first tell them, in his recollection, the events leading to the death of Colin Knight at his home on Woodrow Wilson Drive.

Stokes told his story in chronological fashion, how he and two other men had driven to Knight's home and waited for him to arrive home. When he pulled into his driveway at about one o'clock in the morning on the day of the incident, Stokes said he and the other two men confronted Knight after he got out of his car underneath a carport. Stokes explained the man who hired them to kill Knight wanted them to rough him up first. So they had beaten him almost unconscious and while he lay on the ground next to his car, his accomplices each shot Knight once with their pistols. They made sure he was dead and then left the scene.

"Not that it makes me any less guilty, but I didn't shoot the guy," Stokes said. "I didn't have a gun. But I took part in the beating."

"Will you identify the men who you were with?" Drew asked.

"Dale Shepherd and Buck Miles."

"Associates of yours?"

"We all used to be stunt men and worked on pictures together, but that was a long time ago. None of us have pensions, and we've done some burglaries and other things together since leaving the movie business."

Stokes' story reminded Drew of some other ne'er-do-well ex-stunt men who had turned to crime he had crossed paths with in a previous murder investigation.

"Who paid you to kill Colin Knight?"

"Another actor named Jeremy Taylor. He told us Knight was having an affair with his girlfriend and wouldn't stay away from her. He paid us eight thousand dollars for the job."

"Did you know Taylor from the motion picture business? Is that how he came to offer you the job?"

"No, we had never done that kind of job before. Dale knows this guy named Anthony Fontana from back in New York, but who lives in LA now. Dale says Fontana used to be a mob guy until the FBI turned him into a government witness. Fontana claims he testified against some other mob people and that he's in the witness protection program now. Anyway, Taylor knows him and asked Fontana to kill Knight. But Fontana turned him down because he said he wasn't in that business anymore. Then Fontana told Dale about it and Dale talked to Taylor and took the job."

Drew knew if Fontana was actually in witness protection, it would be tough getting him as a witness because they would need permission from the US Marshals, the agency that handled witness protection. And his actual name wouldn't be Anthony Fontana, but an alias assigned by the government.

"Do you know the name of Taylor's girlfriend?"

"No, he never said."

"Can you tell us where we can find Dale Shepherd and Buck Miles?" Drew asked.

"They both live in Ventura," Stokes said. He gave Drew the address of a mobile home park on Telegraph Road.

"Okay, Woody, I think that about covers it," Drew said. "Someone will transcribe your statement and then we'll be back to get you to sign it. Are you good with that?"

Li switched off the recorder.

"Sure, but don't wait too long to come back, Detective. I don't have much time in this world left."

Drew nodded grimly.

"I've never been a snitch," Stokes said ruefully. "But I'm dying and I can't go with this on my conscience. That's all."

"I understand, Woody, and I appreciate you for doing the right thing by telling us about it."

Drew and Li said goodbye to Stokes and left the room with the chaplain.

"Will you arrest Woody?" the chaplain asked.

"That won't happen," Drew said. "These things take time and it doesn't seem he will be around much longer."

"He won't be," the chaplain said. "So, as Woody said, if having him sign something is important, you shouldn't wait too long to return with it."

Back in the car, Li said, "Well, I couldn't help but feel sympathy for the old guy. But he won't be around to testify."

"No, but a deathbed confession is solid evidence. And now that we have the names of all the other suspects, we should rap this one up pretty quickly."

"See what I mean about actors?" Li said. "They eat their own."

Drew laughed as Li pulled out of the parking lot and they headed back to downtown Los Angeles.

Chapter Thirty-Nine

ON THE WAY BACK TO the PAB, Drew had turned his phone back on and received a call from Melanie Davidson, a union attorney. Davidson agreed to represent Drew and Li and told him she would contact Internal Affairs and the chief's office to notify them she was representing them. Davidson told Drew the department couldn't prevent her from attending any further IAD interviews or meetings with the LAPD brass that discussed disciplinary action. But she warned Drew she wouldn't be able to prevent the department from suspending the detectives because their refusal to cooperate with the Internal Affairs investigators had violated LAPD policy. The department did not recognize all the rights enumerated in the California Public Safety Officers Procedural Bill of Rights Act. But she promised Drew she would do her best. Since he and Li were already in violation of policy, Davidson urged them not to attend any further interviews or make any statements unless she was present.

Drew brought Li up to speed on their representation. He felt happy with Melanie Davidson representing them because she enjoyed a reputation as an accomplished and effective defense attorney. Next, Drew called Lieutenant Moreno, who had tried calling him another five times while Drew had his phone turned off.

"Drew, where the hell are you and Li? Moreno demanded when he answered on the first ring.

"Sorry, Lieutenant, we got an emergency call about the Knight case and had to address it immediately." Drew filled him in on the deathbed confession of Woody Stokes at the Glendale hospice.

"He named the other suspects and told you who paid them to do Knight?" Moreno asked in astonishment, temporarily forgetting the pressing situation with his detectives and IAD.

"Yes, we have it all on tape. We are on our way back to get the recording transcribed and then we'll circle back to him and have him sign the written confession before he dies."

"So, you are about ready to close the case with arrests?"

"Yes, we just have to do the affidavits to get the arrest and search warrants, and then we will pick up the other suspects."

"Okay, good work," Moreno said. Then he remembered why he had been trying to reach Drew. "Drew, I hope you're proud of yourself for raising hell with that stunt you pulled after I left the office. The captain is livid, and so is the deputy chief. You didn't do yourself any favors and I don't know how much you damaged me."

"Lieutenant, whether you believe me or not, the whole thing is bullshit. Kemp is the one in Dunn's pocket protecting him. I was at the trial. Kemp and his informant both made sure Dunn got acquitted on the federal arson-for-hire and insurance fraud case while they buried Dunn's co-defendants. The jury found the other three guilty, and Dunn walked. Dunn is behind this whole thing. He wants us off the Wonderland case."

"That's fine, Drew. I hope what you're saying is true and you all get exonerated. But you've made a bad situation worse for everyone concerned. And I just heard you and Li have lawyered up."

"We would be fools not to. Lieutenant. Look, I do my best to follow policy and follow the rules, but not when they go against common sense. Those IAD stooges read my file after they got those bogus accusations and decided we were guilty. That's how they treated me, and I will not stand by quietly and get railroaded."

"Okay, shut up, and listen, Drew, for one second. The deputy chief talked to the chief and there will be no suspensions for now. You and Li are still off the Wonderland case until further notice. But you will continue working on your other cases."

Moreno took a breath, so Drew took the opportunity to ask a question. "What about Oscar?"

Moreno exhaled audibly. "Estrada also refused to talk to Stanley and Livingston. I guess you have corrupted him along with Li. For now, IAD will continue their investigation and then we go from there after they have finished. But, even if you get exonerated, all three of you will probably be subject to disciplinary action for refusing to comply with policy. Understood?"

"I'm happy right now we aren't getting removed from duty," Drew said. "I'll worry about what comes after we get exonerated because we did nothing wrong and we sure as hell haven't been protecting Dunn. There is nothing for Internal Affairs to find. If they had investigated before they confronted us, none of this would have ever happened."

"All right, Drew. Just get back here and I want a detailed report on Stokes' confession before the end of the day. I want to show it to the captain and maybe he will get off my back for being unable to reach you all day."

"Copy that," Drew said and Moreno disconnected.

"How much trouble are we in?" Li asked.

"Not as much as it could have been," Drew said. He told her about the call with Moreno.

"Well, they aren't suspending us," Li said. "So, that's good. I'm not happy about the threats of disciplinary action after we get cleared of this bullshit. How is that fair? We do nothing wrong and stand up for our rights and they intend to discipline us over a policy violation?"

"Yeah, that's not happening," Drew said. "But we'll fight that battle when we get to it. For now, I'm good with how things are going."

"Well, it's not like we had much time to work the Wonderland case anyway, and we'll stay busy for a while closing out the Knight case."

Li parked the car at the PAB and they headed upstairs to knock out their report before digging into the background of their newly gained suspects in the Knight murder.

Chapter Forty

A FEW WEEKS HAD PASSED since the Internal Affairs detectives had confronted Drew and Li in Moreno's office. Stanley and Livingston hadn't contacted them again since they had got legal representation. As far as Drew knew, the IAD guys were re-interviewing the three individuals who had lodged the accusations against Drew and his team and were comparing their statements against the information the team had recorded in the Wonderland murder books.

Estrada was still working cases with his partner. Drew and Li focused on the Knight case. They had secured arrest warrants and a search warrant for two of the three suspects in the murder-for-hire scheme and had executed the warrants at the mobile home in Ventura rented by the two shooters, Dale Shepherd and Buck Miles. They had arrested Miles and had recovered a hidden Ruger 9-millimeter semi-automatic they believed was one of the murder weapons, but learned Shepherd had fled the Los Angeles area two days before the detectives arrested Miles and was in the wind.

Drew and Li were holding off on arresting Jeremy Taylor until they found more corroborating evidence proving he had hired the three men to kill Colin Knight. Miles had claimed he didn't know Anthony Fontana, the alleged ex-mobster who had referred the job to the three former stunt men, and didn't know where the detectives could find him. The address listed on Fontana's California driver's license record wasn't current and the detectives hadn't yet located him. Woodrow "Woody" Stokes had died nine days after Drew and Li had interviewed him at the Glendale hospice and was out of the picture.

Melanie Davidson, the Protective League attorney representing Drew and Li, had pressured Internal Affairs into handing over the file on the detectives. Drew and Li sat in her office inside the Bradbury Building on South Broadway in downtown Los Angeles, getting their first look at the accusations made against them.

As they already knew, the ATF Agent Jim Kemp was one of their accusers. Kemp had told the IAD detectives that he had talked to Drew, Li, and Estrada on several occasions and provided them with solid leads on the killers involved in the Laurel Canyon murders. He had said that the LAPD detectives had followed up on none of the valuable information he had provided and expressed concern that was because the detectives were actively shielding Tony Dunn and others from arrest and prosecution. Kemp also claimed he had informants inside the Dunn organization who had often seen Drew with Tony Dunn and that they had seemed close, suggesting Detective Drew was one of the many LAPD cops "owned" by Dunn.

When the IAD detectives had asked Kemp if he had anything concrete to back up what he had told them, Kemp had related he had an informant by the name of Billy Van Hoorick who was in federal custody on keep-away status, who had solid information on where the murder weapons were and who had driven the killers and John Watson to the Wonderland house to commit the murders. Kemp claimed Van Hoorick had given the information to the LAPD detectives, which they had also not followed up on.

When asked who the driver was, Kemp stated it was Gina Ramsey, the wife of Terry Ramsey. He explained the Terry Ramsey/Dunn business relationship and how Gina Ramsey was involved in an affair with Dunn at the time of the Wonderland murders. Kemp then gave Detectives Stanley and Livingston contact information for the Ramseys and Van Hoorick and, as the informant's handler, gave them permission to interview him. After the interview, Kemp wanted to know what the IAD detectives would do with the information he had given them. Detective Ian Livingston assured him they would look into the matter and if they discovered corruption or unlawful acts, they would take action.

"How often did you meet with Jim Kemp and what information did he give you?" Davidson asked.

"The only time we every spoke to Kemp was when he came to the office demanding that we turn over all the information we had on Tony Dunn to help him with his federal investigation of Dunn's involvement in an arson and insurance case," Drew replied.

"When Drew told him we wouldn't share information with him, he stormed out of the office," Li added. "He definitely shared no information with us. As Kemp explained it to us, he came to us to get information, not give it."

"The story Kemp gave Internal Affairs is a complete fabrication," Drew said. "We were suspicious Kemp was in Tony Dunn's pocket and had only come to see us on Dunn's behalf to find out if we could tie him to the murders," Drew said. "Kemp was angry when we wouldn't give him what he wanted, but I think it was Dunn who put him up to making the bogus accusations."

"We all attended the federal trial," Li said. "When Kemp testified, he almost left Dunn completely out of the arson and fraud investigation and instead slammed the other three defendants. Kemp was a big part of why the jury convicted those three and acquitted Dunn. Kemp is the one who is probably owned by Tony Dunn."

"Good to know," Davidson said. "I'm preparing a rebuttal to the accusations, which I will give to Internal Affairs and the chief of police." She handed over another sheaf of documents to the detectives. "This is the transcript of the IAD interview of Billy Van Hoorick. Rob Stanley and Ian Livingston drove to San Diego to interview Van Hoorick at the federal detention center after speaking with Kemp."

Drew and Li read the transcript. Van Hoorick told the Internal Affairs detectives that Terry Ramsey, a close associate of Dunn, had good information about the Wonderland murders. He said, according to Ramsey, his wife at the time, Gina Ramsey was shacking up with Dunn and she drove the killers to and from the Wonderland home the day of the murders. According to Van Hoorick, the murder suspects were Justin Carr, a biker named Dennis Mack, and John Watson. He claimed he had given all that information to Detective Drew.

"More fabrications," Drew said, tossing the transcript on the table.

"Did you or anyone on your team interview Van Hoorick?" Davidson asked.

"Early in the case when we were getting hammered with tip line calls, Van Hoorick called from the federal detention center," Drew said. "We had people screening the calls, but whoever got Van Hoorick didn't vet him very well and the call came to me. We talked for maybe ten minutes. He told me nothing close to what the transcript says. He didn't know anymore about the murders than anyone who had access to the papers and television news."

"So, you never went to San Diego to interview him?" Davidson asked.

"No, for two reasons. One he wasn't credible. He told me nothing to show any actual knowledge about the murders. And the other reason is we already had enough problems with the character of the victims and with the witnesses we already had. We didn't need a jailhouse snitch unless it was someone with information that truly passed the smell test. The Ninth Circuit has been overturning convictions left and right on cases that had relied heavily on the testimony of jailhouse informants. On the phone, Van Hoorick didn't impress me as being worth the risk."

"And knowing what we know now," Li added, "Kemp was Van Hoorick's handler, and that makes him even more suspect."

"It seems Kemp told Stanley and Livingston about Van Hoorick to ensure they went to interview him," Davidson said. "Probably because he had already told Van Hoorick what to tell them, so Van Hoorick would corroborate Kemp's story."

"It's also ridiculous that Van Hoorick pointed at Dennis Mack as one of the killers," Drew said. "He's rough around the edges, but he has been one of our most solid witnesses and wants to see Dunn go down as much as we do. Mack helped Joe Allen and Harlan Tate rob Dunn's residence. During the robbery, Mack accidentally shot Justin Carr but only gave him a minor wound, a burn across the back. I doubt sincerely Carr would have used Mack on something like the Wonderland murders, even if Mack would have been willing. And Mack's girlfriend got killed, and he was legitimately grieving her death when we first met him."

Davidson nodded. She replaced the Van Hoorick transcript in the file and pulled out another.

"Before you give it to us to read, I can already guess who the third accuser is," Drew said.

"Who do you think it is?" Davidson asked.

"Terry Ramsey."

"You have a history with him?"

"We interviewed him," Li said. "He told us nothing and threw us out of his dog feces-laden house."

Drew took the transcript and read it with Li. When Stanley and Livingston had interviewed Ramsey, he first pointed out he had been in federal prison at the time of the murders and couldn't have been involved. He then told the detectives his estranged wife, Regina, drove the killers to the Wonderland location to commit the murders. Ramsey said she had used a car registered to him that got repossessed while he was in prison. He also told them Regina had stolen over two hundred thousand dollars from his bail bond business and had given it to Tony Dunn. He had stated further Regina had told him the killers were Dunn, Justin Carr, John Watson, and a guy named Dennis. Ramsey also told the detectives the killers had taken two expensive watches from the victims, Amanda Quinn and Nancy Poole, and that Dunn had given them to a woman named Aayla Campbell, another addict who also lived with Dunn. Ramsey claimed Regina later stole one of the watches from Campbell. Last, Ramsey stated Demond Fabrizia, an employee at Dunn's nightclub called Fiction, received a heroin hot shot while visiting Dunn's home at the behest of Dunn. Ramsey said Detectives Drew, Li, and Estrada had investigated the death and ruled it an accidental overdose to protect Dunn.

When asked by Stanley and Livingston if he had given Detective Drew or any of the other investigators the information about his estranged wife's involvement in the murders, Ramsey admitted he hadn't done so directly. But he told them ATF Agent Jim Kemp also had the same information, and that Kemp had given it to the homicide detectives.

"This would be laughable if it wasn't for the damage they have done to our careers and reputations," Li said after finishing with the third transcript. "It's like they were all reading from the same script."

"Obviously, Kemp was sharing information with Ramsey and coaching his informant on what to say to back up his story," Drew said. "Those assholes from Internal Affairs just took their stories at face value and opened an investigation without verifying any of it."

"From what I've learned, I believe that's accurate," Davidson said. "I think Stanley and Livingston are getting heat from their supervisors for jumping the gun and that's why they are re-interviewing Kemp, Van Hoorick, and Ramsey and trying to confirm their stories after the fact. I'm confident this will all go away soon, although I'm sure this entire episode will still leave an unpleasant taste in your mouths. The department really dropped the ball on this one."

Drew agreed. "My guess is Stanley and Livingston got the stories from Kemp and the others and then read my file. They decided it must all be true, and then only focused on trying to prove what they already believed."

"Well, I'll have my secretary type up your responses and take it to Internal Affairs and the chief's office. I'll call you when I learn anything more. But I'm confident we will beat this."

Chapter Forty-One

BY THE TIME ROB STANLEY and Ian Livingston had completed their investigation, their Internal Affairs case against Drew, Li, and Estrada had collapsed completely. According to their official report, they had determined ATF Agent Jim Kemp had coached his informant and Terry Ramsey with information he had fabricated. They admitted it seemed suspicious a federal agent investigating an organized crime figure like Dunn would share such information with Terry Ramsey, a known felon recently out of prison for attempting to bribe a federal judge. And it was common knowledge Ramsey had an extensive criminal record and was a known associate of the crime figure Kemp was supposed to be investigating.

When Stanley and Livingston had gone back to Kemp's office for a third interview, his supervisor at the Bureau of Alcohol, Tobacco, and Firearms informed them Kemp was under internal investigation for suspected improprieties committed throughout his stint with the Organized Crime Task Force and his association with certain organized crime figures, including Anthony Dunn. Kemp was under suspension.

The interdepartmental report originating from the office of the Commanding Officer, Professional Standards Bureau, authored by Internal Affairs Detectives Stanley and Livingston, and sent to the office of Chief of Police, Los Angeles Police Department, stated in part: "Having completed a review of the Robbery-Homicide Division investigation of which you are aware, our review revealed no indications of previously suggested improprieties and we have closed the case with the determination of unfounded."

The morning after the report arrived on the chief's desk, Drew and Li were at their desks, working on reports, when Lieutenant Moreno walked up to them carrying the Wonderland murder books.

"Where do you want these, Howie?" he asked.

Drew took the stack of blue binders and put them on the shelf above his desk. "We're back on the case?" he asked.

"Well, it seems the accusations were false and the whole thing got blown out of proportion. The captain has reassessed and wants you and Li back on the case, and there will be no disciplinary action taken. That comes down from the tenth floor."

Moreno's tone betrayed his astonishment at the reversal of his detective's fortunes.

"What about the Internal Affairs investigation?" Drew asked.

"Closed as unfounded. Nothing filed on any of you. Like I said, no disciplinary action."

"Lieutenant, I want to tell you something. You told me you did me a favor by bringing me into Homicide Special. I did you a favor by coming here. So, if you're expecting thanks from me, you aren't getting it. I told you it was all bullshit, and I got proven right."

"Drew, I'm not looking for anything from you. You fucked yourself by building the reputation you've had in this department as someone who thinks the rules don't apply to him. The problem is, you may have fucked me when I agreed to accept you into the unit. If it was up to me, you wouldn't get anywhere near this case again."

"But it isn't up to you, is it?" Drew said, turning back to his computer and continuing typing his report without waiting for a reply. Moreno turned and walked back towards his office.

"Howie, I get it," Li said. "I'm as pissed as you are about the way they treated us. But making an enemy out of Moreno isn't smart."

"Fuck, Moreno," Drew said. "He threw us under the bus the first chance he got and he has lost my respect. That isn't what leaders do."

While completing their inquiries, Stanley and Livingston got and served a search warrant at the Bakersfield residence of Regina Ramsey and her common-law husband. As the basis for the warrant, they had used the investigation of the grand theft report taken from her ex-husband, Terry, who had alleged Regina had looted his bail bond business while he was in prison. The items sought with the warrant included jewelry and various documents taken from the safe inside Terry Ramsey's bail bond business office and the watch from one of the female Wonderland victims that Terry alleged his ex-wife had in her possession. They had believed finding the watch could have given validity to the statements her estranged husband had given them. But they didn't find the watch during the search, and in the end no one really believed the watches even existed. But they found enough items in the house from Terry Ramsey's safe to justify the arrest of Regina Ramsey on probable cause for grand theft. They hauled her back to Los Angeles and booked her into Lynwood, known more simply as the Los Angeles County "women's jail." It hadn't been their intention, but the actions of Stanley and Livingston would prove very beneficial to Detectives Drew and Li.

The afternoon of the same day that Moreno had reassigned Drew and Li to the Wonderland investigation, as they were finishing out the day and preparing to leave for home, Drew's phone rang. It was a Lynwood deputy who asked if he knew by the name of Regina Ramsey. Recalling his interview with Terry Ramsey's ex-wife, Drew said he knew her. The deputy told Drew that Ramsey was an inmate and wanted to talk to him about the Wonderland murders.

Drew and Li were at Lynwood within the hour. They signed in and a deputy escorted them to an attorney's conference room to wait for Ramsey. When Ramsey entered, she looked drawn and anxious, about ready to fall apart. She began by telling the detectives she was currently doing the twelve-step program to beat her addiction to cocaine.

"What do you want?" Drew asked impatiently, recalling how Gina Ramsey had stonewalled them when he and Li had interviewed her. "We have no time for any bullshit."

"I'm sorry I wasn't straight with you guys the last time," Ramsey said. "I had some trouble then and was frightened of Tony and just couldn't level with you."

"Fine, now tell us what you want."

"I was at Tony's house on the night of the murders. I had been doing coke most of the day. Justin Carr brought John Watson into the house and he was beating him, trying to find out information about the robbery at Tony's house a few days before. Watson was crying and eventually admitted to Tony that he had set up the robbery with the people over at Wonderland."

"And you witnessed all of it?"

"Yes, but just after Watson confessed, Tony told me to go into the guestroom and stay there. I did, but I stood by the door and could still hear what was going on. I thought they were going to kill Watson, and it scared me to be there."

"So, what did you hear?"

"I heard the doorbell and then Tony greeting others who came into the house. About a minute later, Tony started yelling something like, 'I want them tonight. I want you to kill them all.' I believed he meant the people at the Wonderland house who had robbed him."

"You know who came over? Or how many?"

"I didn't see them because I was already in the guestroom. But at least two guys. I heard them talking."

"Can you tell us anything about them? What they sounded like?"

"I'm only guessing, but Terry and I had a housekeeper for a while, a woman from Haiti. I think they were Haitian, but I'm sure they had Caribbean accents. But different from Tony's. He's Jamaican."

Ramsey looked relieved after she finished the story and hopeful the detectives could do something about the grand larceny charge in return for her helping them.

"I don't know if a case against Dunn will even go to trial," Drew said. "But if it does and you're willing to testify, the district attorney would take your cooperation and testimony into consideration."

"I swear I'll testify. But please help me if you can. I can't go to prison. Without the support I'm getting, I will never beat my addiction."

Drew promised he would do what he could, and then he signaled the deputy they had finished.

Back in their police ride, Li said, "She appeared truthful."

"Sure, but she's still a jailhouse informant looking to benefit."

"Well, it's the closest we've got so far to someone pointing the finger at Dunn."

"Yeah, we've got that going for us," Drew said glumly, starting the car. "I just wish we could get more." Then he pulled out of the parking lot and headed back downtown.

Chapter Forty-Two

THE THIRD ANNIVERSARY of the Wonderland murders came and went. By the end of the year, Dunn had put his home on the market and had moved into a condominium in the San Fernando Valley. He had probably tired of the constant surveillance on the Studio City house and having tenacious cops breaking out his windows and trashing the place during the execution of search warrants.

Terry Ramsey had taken over managing Dunn's Sunset Boulevard nightclub, Fiction, but then Ramsey ran into more legal problems. The investigation into the allegations that Ramsey had bribed the judge to get Dunn's prison sentence reduced had concluded and a grand jury had indicted him. At trial, a jury convicted him and the trial judge sentenced him to the maximum, four years in prison. Ramsey had gone away to begin his second stint in prison, involving bribery of a judicial official.

Deputy DA Alex Douglas had left the district attorney's office and to become a municipal court judge. The district attorney had assigned two new prosecutors to the Wonderland case. Lane Watkins and Erin Hart were both bright and aggressive attorneys, eager to sink their teeth into the case. Watkins was a senior prosecutor with much experience and Hart, while newer, was a talented attorney with two brothers in the LAPD.

Li and Drew had wrapped up the Knight murder case. Juries had returned guilty verdicts at the trials of the two shooters, and both were in prison. Actor Jeremy Taylor, who had paid them to kill Colin Knight, also stood trial, but it ended with a hung jury. The district attorney retried him again but got the same result and Taylor escaped justice, although the district attorney hadn't ruled out trying him a third time.

Moreno had just assigned Drew and Li a new case when Deputy DA Erin Hart called Drew. She told him she and Watkins had finished their review of the Wonderland case and felt the time was right to arrest Tony Dunn for the four murders and the attempted murder. With Regina Ramsey's statement about the night of the murders at Dunn's house locked in, and everything else in place, the prosecution was ready to make their move.

When Drew notified Moreno, expecting the trial might last for weeks, Moreno reassigned the case he had given to Drew and Li so they could focus on rounding up their witnesses and preparing for the trial. Drew contacted the Special Investigation Section and arranged constant surveillance on Tony Dunn as he traveled to and from his new condo in the San Fernando Valley. Thirty-eight months and six days after the Wonderland murders, the arrest warrant issued, Drew and Li sat in the district attorney's office with Watkins and Hart. Li was staying in touch with SIS by phone. It was easier and safer for the cops to take down a potentially armed suspect on the street rather than inside a building. Dunn was at his club in West Hollywood and SIS was ready to take him down.

Time dragged as Drew and Li waited on the call from SIS and both thought about all the scenarios where things could go sideways. Then SIS called and said Dunn was on the move. Soon afterwards, they called back after taking him down without incident on the street just blocks from his club.

Drew and Li met SIS at Hollywood Station and then went into an interview room to talk to Dunn. As soon as they walked into the room, Dunn looked up at them and said, "I have only four words for you, Detectives. I want my lawyer."

Drew turned to Li. "Can you call the prosecutors and let them know he won't talk to us?"

"Sure," Li said, and she stepped out into the corridor to make the call.

With the interview over after Dunn asked for his lawyer, Drew walked over to the switch on the wall and turned off the video recorder.

"You're going down this time, Tony," Drew said.

"Fat chance," Dunn replied sullenly. "I won't get convicted. And even if I do, I'll get out just like last time. I've got better things to do than sit in prison."

Drew smiled, placed his palms on the table, and leaned towards Dunn, who recoiled in his chair.

"Tony, you better hope they convict you, and then you better hope you get life without parole. Either way, if you walk this time or get out of prison early, I'll be waiting. And you will never see me coming."

Li walked back into the room, and Drew stood up straight.

"This detective just threatened me!" Dunn shouted. "I want to file a complaint!"

"You probably just misunderstood him," Li said. Then the detectives walked out and SIS transported Dunn to Men's Central.

Emmitt Wallace, the attorney who had got Dunn's sentence on the narcotics convictions reduced, went back to work at the hearing. He denied Dunn had anything to do with the murders and said the LAPD and the district attorney's office were only trying to save face by arresting his client because they couldn't find the actual killers. He told the judge he was unaware of any new evidence warranting the arrest and argued vigorously for bail.

The prosecutors argued Dunn was a flight risk even if he surrendered his passport and that Dunn was a risk to public safety because of his underworld connections. The judge denied bail and remanded Dunn into custody in the county jail.

Angry at Wallace when he got bound over for trial and denied bail, Dunn fired him and replaced him with two new well-known Los Angeles defense trial lawyers, Kenneth Blackwell and Bradley Willis. Willis had a reputation as a foul-mouthed, anti-cop, anti-death penalty, social justice lawyer who would push the envelope when the trial came around. The local newspaper frequently praised him for his advocacy work in helping the downtrodden, unfairly accused of various crimes by the uncaring, ruthless LAPD cops. Just prior to the start of the trial, the *Times* published a quote from Willis where he said he was "seriously underwhelmed" by the prosecution's case. Kenneth Blackwell clearly was the more self-possessed and deliberative of the two attorneys.

Tony Dunn's trial commenced five months after his arrest, in Department 120 of the Los Angeles Superior Court, Judge Richard Patillo presiding.

Chapter Forty-Three

LI AND DREW SAT IN Lane Watkins' office with Erin Hart on the morning jury selection would take place.

"Do you know where John Watson is?" Hart asked.

"No, we have had no contact with him since his trial," Drew said.

"We have him on the witness list," Hart said. "Lane and I are thinking about subpoenaing him and having him testify."

"To what?"

"When he finally appeared before the grand jury after his acquittal, he made a point of testifying he had only agreed to provide access to the house for the killers because Tony Dunn had threatened to kill him and his family. We think he could help us."

"Can't you just get it in with the grand jury transcript?" Li asked.

"Yes," Watkins said. "But we think it would be more powerful if Watson repeated it from the stand in front of the jury."

"I don't know," Drew said. "John Watson has an extensive history of talking out of both sides of his mouth. There's no telling what he would say in court with Tony Dunn sitting feet away at the defense table."

"We would still like you to find him," Hart said. "Feel him out and see if you can get a read on what we could expect. Then Lane and I will decide."

"All right," Drew said. "You want us to look for him now?"

"Yes, we're working out the order we're putting our witnesses on," Watkins said. "We need to know whether he is in or out."

"We won't finish jury selection today," Hart said. "We will probably finish in the morning and start the trial tomorrow afternoon after lunch."

Drew and Li stood up. "Okay, we'll try to find him."

On the way out of the CCB, Li said. "Any ideas on how to find him?"

"One way would be through talking to Les Emery to see if he knows. He lives up in the San Fernando Valley. We can swing by the office. I've got the address in my notes."

Li and Drew drove to the address in the San Fernando Valley they had for Emery. There was a car in the driveway, but they got no response at the door after knocking several times. Drew felt sure someone was on the other side of the door, looking through the peephole. He could feel them.

"Guess he's not home," Drew said loud enough to ensure whoever was behind the door could hear him. Then he winked at Li.

"Yes, partner. Guess we'll have to come back later."

They walked back and got in their unmarked car. Li did a three-point turn and drove away from the house. At the first intersection, she made a U-turn and stopped at the curb down the street, where they had a view of the front of Emery's home. The detectives had a little time to kill and sometimes these things paid off.

About fifteen minutes passed and then they saw Les Emery walked out the front door and hurry to his car. Li sped forward and stopped their car in the street, blocking Emery's driveway. The detectives got out and strode toward his car.

"What's this about?" Emery asked gruffly.

"We're looking for John Watson and figure you're the person to ask, Les," Drew replied.

"John doesn't work for me anymore. He's out of the business."

"Doesn't mean you don't know where he is," Li said.

"What do you want him for this time?"

"We only want to talk," Drew said. "He isn't in any trouble."

"Well, that's good," Emery said. "He's not well."

"What's his problem?" Li asked.

"He hasn't told me, but I think he contracted AIDS."

"That doesn't sound good," Drew said. "You know where he is?"

"Sepulveda Veterans Hospital the last I heard. His new wife, Lola, called me."

"Les, did John ever tell you anything about what happened up on Wonderland the night of the murders?" Dew asked.

"Nothing," Emery replied curtly. The accompanying glare told the detectives they had just heard all they would ever hear from Emery on the subject. Pornographic film maker Les Emery had finally dumped Watson when his drug habit grew so bad Watson could no longer perform. Business was business. But he still supported Watson in private and public.

After calling the Sepulveda Veterans Medical Center and confirming John Watson was a patient there, Li and Drew drove to the hospital on Plummer Street in North Hills, a community in the north-central San Fernando Valley region of Los Angeles.

They found Watson in bed in a small single room at the end of a large ward. A woman, they soon learned, was his new wife Lola was there with him. Li and Drew later agreed they had seen dead people who looked in better shape than John Watson. He appeared emaciated with scraggly hair and a beard, and his fingernails were exceptionally long. Watson appeared to weigh about a hundred pounds and various sized ulcerated splotches were present on his face, arms, and hands.

Watson greeted them with a simple, "Hey, guys," as if they were old friends he had expected to visit.

"Hey, John," Drew said. "We heard you were ill and thought we would stop by to see how you were doing."

"Well, my fingernails hurt, but I'm okay, I guess. You know, I really need a smoke, but they won't let me smoke in here. You guys mind going outside with me to talk?"

"Sure, John, whatever you need," Drew said.

Lola helped Watson into a wheelchair. From the looks of it, both detectives realized he could no longer walk. They followed behind as Lola rolled Watson outside to a smoking area. He lit a cigarette and took a puff.

Watson began the conversation by making small talk, and then he did what he had always done, talk out of both sides of his mouth. He carried on about how bad he felt because of the way things turned out. While he had wanted to help the detectives with their investigation, he had needed time to think things through.

It was obvious to Drew that Watson might expire any day and so he didn't bother telling Watson what they had actually come to see him about. There was no way Watson could have attended court, even if he had wanted to. So, he quickly wrapped up the visit, after Watson said he was tired and needed to go back to his room to rest. Drew wished Watson luck even though he didn't mean a word of it.

"You guys come back in a few days," Watson said. "I'll have everything written down about what went down up at Wonderland for you. If I'm not around, Lola will have it for you."

"Sure, John, that would be great," Drew said, not believing a word of it.

As Lola pushed Watson back towards his room, Drew and Li headed for the hospital exit.

"He looks like he is already dead," Li said.

"Poetic justice," Drew said. "At least when he goes, they won't need many pallbearers at the funeral."

"Why? Because he's lost so much weight?"

"Garbage cans have only two handles," Drew said.

Chapter Forty-Four

THE TRIAL OF ANTHONY "Tony" Dunn did not draw anywhere near the amount of media attention that the John Watson trial had drawn some years earlier. The media had found Watson, with his sordid past, getting put on trial far more alluring than when it happened to an unknown thug.

In her opening statement, Deputy District Attorney Erin Hart described the robbery at Dunn's home and established the violent incident had motivated the revenge killings at Wonderland. She mentioned the name of each victim and articulated the savage injuries suffered by Dawn Allen. Hart concluded her remarks by stating the prosecution would prove that the defendant had ordered the horrific attacks on the sleeping victims inside the house on Wonderland Avenue. She had given a strong opening that was to the point.

Bradley Willis handled the opening statement for the defense. He told the jurors his client lived in a world devoid of the value system that they knew. Then he told them, although his client had lived in the world of drugs by choice, he was innocent of the charges and that the LAPD and the district attorney's office had conspired to arrest and charge his client to cover up their incompetence and inability to identify those responsible for the murders and attempted murder of Dawn Allen. Willis promised the defense would name the actual killers of the people at Wonderland before the trial ended and would prove his client had not been involved.

As it usually happened in murder trials, the first witness called by the prosecution were law enforcement types. This included the investigative personnel from the Scientific Investigation Division and the criminalists who had collected, analyzed, and preserved the evidence from the crime scene. Next came the investigating detectives, and once again Howard Drew testified first as he had in the Watson trial.

Drew related what he and his fellow detectives had observed and discovered in the way of victims and evidence. He then introduced the videotaped walk-through of the bloody crime scene, where he had narrated descriptions of the brutally beaten victims and the various items of evidence found and collected. The jurors saw in vivid and graphic detail just how brutal the attacks had been. As in the Watson trial, there were gasps and other emotional expressions from the jurors and courtroom spectators.

The first civilian witness the prosecutors called was Dennis Mack. He sported a long gray beard and testified with the same steely eyed expressions as before. In what Drew thought was a brilliant move, Hart led Mack through his long and violent past of drug arrests, robbery, assaults, and burglary so as not to leave his criminal history for the defense to exploit. Once his sordid past was in front of the jury, Hart had Mack describe the Dunn robbery in detail. At the end of his testimony, Mack admitted he and the Wonderland crew had gotten in over their heads when they had ripped off Dunn. "There are certain dope dealers you don't rob," Mack said, "and one of them was Mr. Dunn."

Bradley Willis cross-examined Mack. His favored tactic was a common one for defense attorneys. Put the witnesses on trial, not the defendants. And he wasted no time with Mack. "Isn't it true you called yourself a robber when asked your profession at the trial of John Watson?" Mack replied without hesitation.

"I think we've established I'm not a very nice guy, and I lie sometimes. But no matter what I've done, I've never killed anybody. He did." Mack pointed at Tony Dunn.

Willis shouted an objection. Judge Patillo sustained the objection and instructed the jury to disregard Mack's remark and gesture. He admonished Mack to only answer the questions asked, but things got no easier for the defense as Mack brooked no nonsense from Willis throughout the cross-examination, which lasted several hours. As experienced and aggressive an attorney as he was, had it been a boxing match, Mack would have won by a knockout.

As criminal trials progress with multiple attorneys on each side, while one attorney is examining or cross-examining witnesses, the others on both sides observe the jury. They looked for signs of inattention, bias, nervousness, or anything that might reveal which way a juror might be leaning. That was true of the Dunn trial. And for some time, the prosecuting attorneys had already noticed that eighteen-year-old juror Nasheya Washington from South Central Los Angeles appeared disinterested, never took notes, and had no interaction with the other jurors when they were on breaks or were entering or leaving the courtroom. Both Watkins and Hart shared the opinion that the young juror seemed biased either against the prosecution or toward Tony Dunn, and worried she would be a problem when the case went to the jury.

During the lunch break, after Mack finished testifying, Drew and Li went to the courthouse cafeteria to grab a bite and some coffee. As they exited the line after paying, they both narrowly missed bumping into Nasheya Washington. Drew made a sudden side step, followed by Li. She glared at them both. Since the rules prohibited them from speaking with any juror, Drew smiled at her apologetically and Li gave her a friendly nod. In return, Washington flashed them another angry glare the like of which the detectives would not have even given Tony Dunn. Nasheya Washington did not like them and probably did not like cops at all. They both knew that was not a good sign.

After the trial recessed for the day. Drew and Li met with the prosecutors in the district attorney's office. Drew shared with them about the run in with juror Nasheya Washington in the courthouse cafeteria.

"Yes, Lane and I have already discussed her," Hart said. "We weren't comfortable with her from the start, but by the time we got to her we had used all of our preemptive challenges and had no cause to disqualify her."

"I'd hate to see the trial go smoothly only for Dunn to walk on a mistrial when one cop-hating juror hangs the jury," Drew said.

"We will monitor her," Watkins said. "If she continues sitting in the box with her arms crossed and that bored expression on her face, we will speak to the judge."

Drew nodded his agreement, but already thought it time for some preemptive action.

Chapter Forty-Five

DURING THE SECOND WEEK of the trial, Erin Hart called Regina Ramsey to the stand. Ramsey related the story about the robbery at Dunn's house, the alleged motivation behind the murders. Next, Hart led her through the entire scenario where Justin Carr forced John Watson into Dunn's home for the up close and personal discussion with Dunn. Hart also delved into Ramsey's history, her association with Tony Dunn and her addiction to cocaine. Then the prosecutor asked Ramsey what she had heard from behind the closed door of the guestroom on the first floor of Dunn's home when Dunn and Carr had John Watson out in the living room.

"Carr and Dunn were beating Mr. Watson up," Ramsey said. "They wanted information from him about the robbery at the house that happened a few days before. I overheard Dunn tell Mr. Watson that if he didn't take him to those people that robbed him, he would have every member of his family killed."

"Did you hear the defendant say anything else about the people who had robbed him?" Hart asked.

"He said he would have them all on their knees and would teach them a lesson and they would never steal from him again."

"Do you recall a conversation with the defendant after the murders while you were freebasing cocaine together?"

"Yes," Ramsey acknowledged.

"Tell us about the conversation."

"Mr. Dunn became upset while under the influence of the coke and he told me, 'Things had gone too far. It turned into a bloody mess.' Then, after he said it, he told me that people had the habit of disappearing in the canyon and that if I ever talked about anything to anyone, he would have every tooth in my head pulled and my hands cut off so no one could identify my body."

"Did that frighten you?"

"Yes, very much so. That's when I knew I had to get away from him. The first chance I got, I left the house and then left LA for Bakersfield."

Dunn's attorney, Bradley Willis, cross-examined Ramsey and went for her throat.

"Isn't it true you made a deal with the district attorney's office to testify in this trial just to avoid prosecution on a pending grand larceny charge?"

"I have a pending charge, but no one promised me anything for testifying. I'm trying to do the right thing."

"Oh come now, Ms. Ramsey. Didn't you concoct a bunch of lies and make everything up you've testified to after reading about the murders in the papers?"

The attorney's assault shook Ramsey, but she denied the accusations.

"No, that's a lie. Everything I've said was the truth."

Willis' vicious attacks and Ramsey's denials went on for over an hour longer. The attorney had shaken her and scored some points. But by the time Willis finished his cross- examination, Drew figured most of the people in the courtroom saw Willis as a cruel bully and felt sympathetic towards Ramsey.

Dunn had appeared attentive during her testimony but was also fuming. Drew was unsure whether he was angry with Ramsey or his attorney's inability to impeach her testimony completely. It was the prosecution's strongest evidence that Dunn had ordered the Wonderland murders.

The prosecution called several other witnesses to testify after Ramsey. Willis attacked them all from every conceivable angle. However, when Watkins called Dawn Allen to the stand, the defense backed off. It would have been foolish for them to go after a woman who had got beaten within an inch of her life and who still had multiple medical issues. Her testimony was vague anyway, much the same as in the Watson trial. The prosecutors felt she held back on her recollections out of fear of Dunn, and if so, Drew thought it was probably understandable. Kenneth Blackwell took the cross and handled her gently. He asked only a few questions and seemed satisfied once he got her to admit she had not seen his client in the house when she suffered the assault.

Seven weeks after the trial began and one month and three weeks before the fourth anniversary of the Wonderland murders, the case against Tony Dunn ended and went to the jury.

Drew had been digging into the background of juror Nasheya Washington. Her behavior in the courtroom hadn't undergone a positive change. And a few days after the case went to the jury, Drew found two interesting pieces of information. A little over two years before, two Central Division patrol cops had shot and killed her brother Antonne Washington during a foot pursuit when Washington had turned and fired a shot at them. The Force Investigation Division had subsequently cleared them, finding they had acted within policy.

Since age sixteen, Nasheya Washington had worked as a paid activist for the South Central Coalition Against Police Abuse community organization. The organization's stated aim was organizing marginalized groups in South Central to prevent, expose, and resist police abuse, to seek legal redress for such abuse, and to lobby for defunding the LAPD.

Drew and Li drove over to the district's attorney's office to inform Watkins and Hart of Drew's findings. The detectives hadn't attended the voir dire because they had been out looking for John Watson. But Drew knew one question commonly asked during selection for a criminal trial was whether a past interaction or experience with the police had caused the person to form an opinion about the police or the criminal justice system that would prevent them from being a fair juror. Drew felt a keen interest in learning how Nasheya Washington had answered the question.

Watkins and Hart were on their way out of the office when the detectives arrived.

"We need to talk," Drew said.

"Can it wait?" Watkins asked. "Judge Patillo just summoned us to his chambers. The jury foreman sent him a note that there was a problem with a juror. We were just headed downstairs."

Quickly Drew told them what he had uncovered about Nasheya Washington.

"Oh, shit," Hart said. "I had a feeling she was the juror the foreman wants to talk to the judge about. I asked her the bias against the police or criminal justice system question and I remember she said no. You better come with us."

The detectives followed the prosecutors downstairs to Patillo's chambers. Once they arrived in the outer office, Watkins told the detectives to wait outside and he would come and get them if the judge wanted to speak to them.

Both defense attorneys were already in the room with Judge Patillo when Watkins and Hart walked in.

"All right, good," Judge Patillo said, sitting behind his desk. "The jury foreman has contacted me about a problem with one of the other jurors. Eleven of the jurors agree on a verdict with one holdout."

"Sounds like we have a hung jury, Your Honor," Bradley Willis said. "Of course, we prefer a not guilty verdict because our client is innocent. But under the circumstances, we respectfully move for a mistrial."

"Hold on, Mr. Willis," Patillo said. "I haven't finished. The juror in question refuses to deliberate or review the evidence. The foreman feels the dissenting juror reached a decision before the trial started and won't be swayed. And when other jurors expressed their impatience, the holdout made statements to the effect that the police cannot be trusted because they lie and plant evidence. Sounds like a straightforward case of bias to me."

"Have you interviewed the juror, Your Honor?" Willis asked, suddenly grasping that the holdout was all that stood in the way of a guilty verdict for his client. "Only seems fair that they get the chance to give their side of the story."

"I haven't spoken with them," Patillo said. "But I intend to. I only wanted to inform counsel of the issue before proceeding. If the foreman has exaggerated the situation, then I'll ask them to continue deliberating and to try to break the deadlock. But if I get a sense there is bias, I'll dismiss the juror and replace them with an alternate and we will continue."

"Your Honor," Hart said. "Not to assume I know which juror you've spoken about, but I just received some information that may be relevant."

"What kind of information, Ms. Hart?"

"Evidence that one juror was untruthful during voir dire, Your Honor, and it goes to bias."

The judge leaned his elbows on the desk and placed his face in his hands for a moment. "All right," Patillo said, looking back up at the attorneys. "Ms. Hart, without naming the juror, explain."

"There is a juror who gave a no response when I asked if an experience or interaction left them biased against the police or the criminal justice system.

I have learned the juror had a brother shot and killed by police officers in South Central two years ago and for the past two years has worked as a paid activist for South Central Coalition Against Police Abuse, your garden variety anti-police community organization."

Patillo nodded gravely. "Step out please, and I'll speak to the juror. Then I'll call you all back in after I decide."

The two defense attorneys and the prosecutors stepped out into the outer office and Watkins closed the door behind them. Willis glared at Drew and Li when he saw them standing in the office, but didn't speak when Blackwell placed a hand lightly on his arm.

Twenty minutes later, Patillo called the attorneys back in. He informed them he had dismissed Nasheya Washington from the jury and replaced her with an alternate juror. He told them the deliberations would continue.

Chapter Forty-Six

AFTER JUDGE PATILLO had recused the biased juror and replaced her with an alternate, the jury reached a unanimous verdict the following day. They found Anthony Dunn guilty on the four counts of first degree murder and one count of attempted murder. Drew respected the tough decision made by Judge Patillo. Drew knew and was sure that the judge knew Dunn's attorneys would appeal because of his decision, since there had been a conviction. But at least for the time being, the murder victims and Dawn Allen had received a measure of justice. Tony Dunn's conviction and the three brass verdicts Drew had rendered on Carr and his crew. He figured they had got all the suspects except John Watson.

Once the jury foreman had read the verdict, Drew and Li left the courtroom and returned to the PAB to close out the Wonderland case. At five o'clock, Li told him she had to meet someone and asked if they could have a celebratory drink later. Drew told her, sure, he wasn't in the mood to celebrate anyway. She wished him a good evening and left. Drew stayed behind to make the last updates to the murder book chronologies.

Lieutenant Moreno walked through on his way out and stopped at Drew's desk. "I heard about the verdict, Detective," he said. "Congratulations. It was a good case, Drew. Really good police work."

"Coming from you, Lieutenant, that means a lot."

Moreno looked at him with narrowed eyes. He wasn't sure if Drew had just insulted him. Moreno cleared his throat.

"Anyway, I was just going to drop off a message for you on the way out."

Moreno looked down at a slip of paper in his hand.

"A woman named Lola said to tell you John died. Mean anything to you?"

"John Watson," Drew said. "Lola was his new wife. He got AIDS. Not sure what John told her, but she must have thought we were friends or something to call. Like I give a shit. Good riddance."

"Well, I guess that's the last of everyone involved in the murders."

"Yeah. I'd rather have seen everyone go to prison. But I'll take it."

"Listen, Howie. About before..."

"Don't worry about it," Drew interrupted.

"Don't worry about it? You're staying here in Homicide Special. Neither of us can do anything about that. I think we need to clear the air to ensure we can work together going forward."

"I can't help you there, Lieutenant. It's not my call. So, as far as the IAD fiasco, don't worry about it. I'm trying to do you a favor, man."

"I'm not talking about the ill-intentioned IAD investigation, Drew. What I'm saying is nothing has changed my mind about your behavior. The way you act like the department policies don't apply to you."

"You don't trust me much, do you, Lieutenant?"

"In matters of subordinates going off like a loose cannon, I don't trust anyone. I'm a fair man, Drew. And I'm willing to let bygones be bygones. But I want to know what I can expect from you going forward."

"You can expect me to show up on time for work every workday, Lieutenant. You can expect me to give my best efforts toward closing every case you hand off to me. And you can expect me to take the weight if I ever fuck up. But here is what you can't expect. Don't expect me to lie down and take it if Internal Affairs or anyone else in this department tries to steamroll me over some bullshit I didn't do."

"You know something, Drew. Your problem is you don't understand how it works. You don't understand the department is always more important than any individual. Cops come and cops go, but the department will always survive. The same can't be said of an individual who refuses to follow policy when it doesn't suit him."

"Are you afraid?" Drew asked.

"Afraid of what, Detective?"

"Of me. Yourself. Of everything. Are you afraid you might be wrong and I might be right? Aren't you afraid everything you have ever believed about this department is wrong?"

"The only thing I fear is people who act without thinking their actions through, Detective. And that's how you behaved in my office with Stanley and Livingston, knowing you were violating department policy. You aren't a team player. You play for yourself."

Drew just shook his head. Moreno was too embroiled in the politics and couldn't see outside the bubble he willingly occupied.

"Just what it is you want, Detective? What is it you expect from me so we can put this all behind us so I can feel comfortable trusting you going forward?"

"I expect nothing from you," Drew said. "Not after that day in your office with those two IAD clowns. Trust goes both ways."

Moreno shrugged in resignation. "I really don't understand you, Drew," he said. Then he walked to the door, went out, and closed the door behind him.

After dinner, Drew and Melanie Davidson exited El Compadre, the Silver Lake Mexican restaurant that was one of Drew's favorites. He walked the attorney to the parking lot. They had arrived in separate cars. They had run into each other again at the CCB and had coffee together. To his surprise, he had asked her out to dinner and it surprised him even more when she had accepted. Davidson had worn a simple black dress that showed her attractive figure and highlighted her shoulder-length blond hair. He had spoken with Nina Garraway and confirmed things were over. She had told him she wanted to keep things on just a professional basis. Given their respective professions, they both knew they would see each other often.

"I guess I should go," she said after they had been silent for several moments.

Drew nodded and backed away.

"Thank you for the lovely dinner, Howie."

He nodded again. "My pleasure. Thanks for coming."

Now she nodded and turned to walk to her car.

"You like country western?" Drew asked.

She stopped and turned back to him. There was a sharpness in her eyes, but a softness in her expression that told Drew of a need for touch. It was so clear he could feel it.

"Some of it," she said. "The modern stuff."

"There is... there is a concert at Marina Green in Long Beach this weekend. The Coastal Country Jam on Saturday evening. Priscilla Block, a new singer I really like, is performing. I mean, if you don't think it's too soon to ask you out again."

Melanie walked back to him and put a hand behind his neck, pulling his face down to hers. He surrendered willingly. They kissed for a long time. When she pulled away, he didn't look to see if anyone was watching. He didn't care.

"I don't think it's too soon," she said. "Do you?"

Drew shook his head.

"Call me and let me know when you're picking me up on Saturday."

He smiled. She smiled back.

She turned again and walked to her car, her high heels clicking on the pavement. Drew leaned back against his car and watched her get in. He returned her wave and smile as the BMW M2 coupe passed by him. Then he lit a cigarette and watched as the sleek white machine turned onto Sunset Boulevard and left him standing in the parking lot alone, wondering if it was too soon.

Also by Larry Darter

A Jacob Dedman Novel
The Dedman Emergence

Howard Drew Novels
Omerta
Darker Angels
LA Deadly
Laurel Canyon
The Pendulum

Malone Mystery Novels
Come What May
Fair Is Foul and Foul Is Fair
Cold Comfort
Foregone Conclusion
Foul Play
Black Deeds
Perchance To Dream
Malone Mystery Novels Box Set: Come What May, Fair Is Foul and Foul Is
Fair, Cold Comfort
Live Long Day

Rich Bishop Novels
Follow the Money
China Doll

Rick Bishop Novels
The Girl on the Beach
Dead End
Trouble in Paradise

T. J. O'Sullivan Series
Mare's Nest
Honolulu Blues
The Chinese Tiger Ying
Frisky Business
Missing Time

Standalone
All Our Yesterdays
Malone Mystery Novels Two Book Set No. 1

Watch for more at www.larrydarter.com.

About the Author

Larry Darter is an American author best known for his crime fiction novels written about the fictional private detective Malone. He is a former U.S. Army infantry officer, and a retired law enforcement officer. He lives with his family in Oklahoma.

Read more at https://www.larrydarter.com.

www.ingramcontent.com/pod-product-compliance
Lightning Source LLC
Chambersburg PA
CBHW032004240626
47153CB00003B/1123